How To Be
A Better
Adult

Jacque Aye

Cover art: Odunze Oguguo

Cover design: Jacque Aye

CHAPTER 1

—— ◆ ——

THE THIRD FLOOR

The third floor of William Hensley & Associates was shrouded in dimness. Dimness because it wasn't quite pitch-black darkness but rather a dreary gray. The dark window shades were tightly drawn, and fluorescent lights flickered overhead, teasing the third-floor employees with a few brief moments of illumination before the gloom set back in. The only constant source of light was the dull glow of computer screens.

Black-clad employees sat at cramped cubicles before their screens, working with their heads down and speaking in hushed whispers—when they did speak. But most times, they worked in silence. The gentle click-clacking of computer keys and scritching of pencil to paper was the only sound to be heard.

In the dimness, at a corner cubicle, sat Hope Obiako. Hope was a small woman with an equally small demeanor—although she would beg to differ. Her kinky hair was pulled tightly into a neat bun, and her crisp slacks were starched to perfection. On the bridge of her nose sat a pair of round-framed glasses that she didn't need to see but rather to appear well-read. And she *was* well-read—she *just needed everyone else to know it.*

Hope glanced at the calendar on her desk, eyeing the day's red-marked appointment.

It's almost time, she thought, her heart pounding in anticipation. She cleared the nervousness from her throat and took a sip of cold tea from her mug.

Buzzz!

Hope jumped a bit in her seat. She'd forgotten to switch her cell phone to silent. This was a mortal sin on the third floor, as phones were banned for being "unsensible tools of distraction". Hope fumbled with her desk drawer as each vibration grew louder than the last, piercing the silence that blanketed the office.

A loud, sharp "Shhhh!" shot through the air, followed by chair creaks and rustling papers. Someone was getting upset. Heat rose to Hope's cheeks, and her palms slipped with sweat, making it even harder to find that pesky phone. Finally, she spotted it, hidden underneath a pile of post-it notes. Hope grabbed the phone with her slippery hand, trying not to drop it, and quickly hung up. The missed call was from her landlady, Lisa. She knew it was only a matter of time before she'd receive a text message reminding her to pay her rent.

"Hey, Hope!" A whispered voice shot around the corner of Hope's cubicle.

Hope winced at the sound of her name. It'd been a while since she'd been directly spoken to at work. She leaned back in her rolling chair and peeked over to see her cubicle neighbor Alex staring back at her. Alex had a kind of pleasant face that always seemed to be smiling, even when he wasn't. He sat up straight, but not *too* straight, and casually commanded the respect of a seasoned executive, although he was quite young. His brown eyes gleamed through the dimness, and his dark hair was parted and slicked like a nineteen-fifties car salesman.

Hope held up her cell phone and mouthed, "sorry".

"You're fine!" He swatted away Hope's apology. "I was actually gonna ask you for a favor, but you look really busy today," he whispered.

Hope swelled with pride. She couldn't help it. He said she looked not just busy, but *really* busy. He must have noticed her glancing at her calendar. Or maybe it was the tea. *No, no, it was definitely the calendar.*

"A bit. But not too busy to help out a cubicle neighbor!" She flashed a toothy grin, which he returned. "What do you need?"

"Well...could you please grab me another cup of coffee? *Thanks!*" He thrust his empty, coffee-stained mug into her hands and swiveled back to face his work.

Hope sat in her embarrassment for a moment, racking her brain for something, anything to say to save face and snatch her shreds of power back. She imagined rolling over to Alex and letting him know she was far too busy to run errands like some kind of lowly assistant. She thought of simply placing the mug on her desk and returning to her calendar without acknowledging its audacious presence in her workspace. But instead, she responded to Alex's back with an enthused, "Sure!".

Hope mentally kicked herself for being a pushover and stood to make the trek to the break room at the other end of the floor.

The third floor felt more like a labyrinth than a corporate office. The layout was so haphazard that one could only assume the interior designer, architect, or whoever deals with such things as cubicle arrangement had been laughed out of business.

Not all the blame could be placed on their shoulders, however. The low light was actually a preference of Liz, the third-floor manager. She thought having employees squint and hunch over their work would make them produce more efficiently. But in reality, they resembled evil henchmen, crafting dastardly plans in the dark. As you can imagine, this didn't do much to lift the third floor's waning morale.

Hope checked her watch. It was nine-forty-five. She quickened her pace. She didn't want to be away from her desk for too long. It was nearly time for her appointment.

The break room housed a giant, glowing, state-of-the-art coffee machine. Liz was a fan of cutting corners, but when it came to coffee, W&H employees were provided the cream of the crop. They had to stay alert and awake to work, after all.

Hope dispensed fresh black coffee into Alex's mug, then scurried out of the break room. On her way out, she bumped into a small woman, nearly spilling on her. Instead, the scalding coffee splashed onto Hope's hand, which she had used to shield her near-victim from the hot liquid.

"I'm so sorry!" Hope whispered to the woman as she winced in pain and wiped her wet, hot hand on her pant leg.

Unfortunately for Hope, the little woman she'd bumped into was Monica, the head of HR. Usually, Monica worked on the seventh floor, so her presence was an unpleasant surprise. There she stood, with her mouth gaping open and her arms outstretched, with a pen in one hand, like the humanized version of the saying, "you've gotta be kidding me".

"You've *got to* be kidding me!" she whispered. "Did you spill that on me?"

Hope examined her throbbing, red palm, then looked Monica up and down. From her atrocious red bob with gaudy blonde highlights down to her tacky shoes, there was not a single drop of coffee on her pristinely plain being.

"No. You're fine."

"Geez, I just bought this skirt last week." Monica sharply exhaled and wiped imaginary coffee off of her white skirt.

"There's nothing there," Hope assured her.

"You definitely spilled on me." Monica sighed. "I can't believe this," she griped as she continued wiping.

Hope had dealt with people like Monica enough to know that she was putting on a show to receive sympathy of some sort. And for that very reason, she wasn't going to give in.

"Mix vinegar with water and spray it on the stain. It'll lift right up!" Hope recalled a handy tidbit she'd read while browsing the web.

Monica stopped fussing with her skirt and glared at her.

"Thanks for the tip." Her eyes moved from Hope to the coffee cup. "What are you doing with Alex's mug anyway?"

Hope examined the nondescript mug in her hand.

Monica shot Hope with an accusatory look that made her uncomfortable. "Does he know you have it?"

"Yes," Hope clenched her jaw and gripped the mug tighter, "I'm grabbing coffee for him…"

"Hm. Well, I'll let you get back to that," Monica hissed dismissively. "And all's forgiven for the coffee spill. Ok?" She slit her eyes and flashed a patronizing smile, bestowing her forgiveness upon her like some precious jewel.

"Ok, see you around!" Hope returned her smile for the sake of office politics, and because her entire career and livelihood could be ended with one stroke of the pen in Monica's tiny, manicured fingers.

Back at her cubicle, Hope handed Alex his half-spilled coffee. "Here you go!"

"Thanks. You're the best!" Alex grabbed the mug without looking up from his computer screen.

Hope fumed...in her head, of course. In reality, she responded to the slight with a pathetic "you're welcome" and plopped back into her chair, defeated.

♡♡♡

Click clack.

Click clack.

A shadowy figure with obnoxiously noisy shoes approached Hope's cubicle. The shadow was a woman. A tall, lanky woman with bony hips that jutted as she walked, and pale gray skin that perfectly blended into the gloomy atmosphere. Her steely bob whipped her cheekbones as she darted her head from side to side, peering over cubicles, ensuring that everyone was indeed working.

"And what are *you* working on?" The woman stood behind her now, her tall willowy body towering over Hope's tiny, seated frame.

"Hello, Liz." With her glasses on and pages of notes strewn across her desk, Hope appeared knee-deep in some pressing matter.

She was very proud of herself. "I'm preparing for our meeting this morning."

"Our...*meeting*?"

"Uh, yes, you sent me a meeting invite a few days ago..."

"What's your name?"

"It's Hope? Obiako. Remember?" Hope's voice cracked just a bit.

"No." Liz checked her smartwatch. "But there does seem to be an appointment blocked off on my calendar. So, let's get this over with."

Hope had been waiting her entire year-long "career" for this moment. Before this week, the only meeting she'd ever been called into was with the Employee Morale Committee to discuss changing the paint color in the women's bathroom. She'd chosen a seafoam green. More specifically, a shade called "Sea Maiden", which she'd read was an excellent mood booster. They thanked her, and the next week the walls were a darker shade of their usual gray.

This meeting would be different, though. *This* meeting had an exclamation point attached to the email invite. A glowing red exclamation point, in fact. It was *urgent,* and Hope knew that urgency was reserved for very important matters.

Liz effortlessly whipped through the cubicle maze, throwing intimidating looks at hunched-over employees. Hope followed, fine-tuning her professional demeanor on the way. Chest high, chin up. She'd read about the power of posture in a book. She couldn't quite remember what it was called or who had written it, but the cover was green. Or maybe it was blue. *No, it was definitely green.*

No, it was blue, she thought as she straightened her back and firmly gripped the handle of her briefcase.

As the pair reached Liz's office, Hope felt a lump hardening in her throat.

I can do this, she thought, shaking away her nerves. *I'm capable. I'm charming. People like me.* It was a mantra her therapist, Dr. Marley, had made her repeat until she claimed to believe it. She remembered the session like it was yesterday—because it was.

"*I'm capable. I'm charming. People like me.*"

"Now say it again." Dr. Marley demanded while leaning forward on his stool, his wild curls contrasting with his dull, droopy eyes. "But like you mean it. *Mean it,* Hope."

Hope forced a smile. "I'm capable. I'm charming. People like me."

"Why do people like you?"

"Because...I'm capable and charming?"

"Do you believe that?"

Hope paused for a moment, taking some time to pull at a loose thread in her jeans.

Dr. Marley's eyes sunk even further into his skull as he let out a heavy sigh in frustration. "If you continue to hold onto these false beliefs about yourself, I'll be forced to extend our sessions—"

"I do. I do believe it." Hope declared without lifting her head. Extended sessions meant more money spent, as Dr. Marley charged by the minute.

A smile crept across Dr. Marley's face, lifting the heavy bags that hung from his eyes.

"I believe it, Dr. Marley." Hope nodded her head with conviction. Of course, she didn't believe it, but at least the lie made him happy. No sense in both of them being miserable, really.

"I'm capable. I'm charming. People like me."

Seven mantras later, Hope found herself standing in Liz's office for the first time in a year. Unlike the rest of the floor, her office was extremely well-lit. It was almost *too* bright, like the sterile glow of a hospital.

Liz slid behind her tall alabaster desk, which towered over a tiny black chair.

"Have a seat..." she insisted, motioning towards the chair, "...while I figure out why you're here."

Hope took her seat, paying close attention to her posture. She sat up straight, kept her shoulders relaxed and open, crossed her legs, and let her hands gently lay on the armrests beside her. She stopped herself from nervously wiggling her foot.

Liz tapped her long talon-like fingernails on the desk, almost impatiently, as she read through emails.

"Ah, here we are." She peered down at Hope. "How do you feel about your career here at William Hensley & Associates?"

"I love it here. It's such an amazing atmosphere." Hope lied. "I'm proud to be part of this company."

The latter was true and was the reason she, or anyone else for that matter, stayed put. A certain level of prestige came with the title of William Hensley & Associate employee. And that prestige came at a lofty price for many of its employees.

Liz scribbled something on a pad beside her.

"Are you happy with your workload?"

"Yes. I'm quite busy. The work is challenging, but I'm more than capable, and I believe I contribute a lot to this great company." Hope lied again.

"What about your co-workers? Do you feel you've had an opportunity to bond with them and work together as a team?"

"Oh yes, of course." Another lie.

Liz raised a thinly drawn eyebrow before continuing. "I'm told you've been a great addition to the William Hensley team. Especially here on the third floor." She sounded rehearsed, like she was reading a script for a play she didn't want to be in.

Hope brushed away her tone. She was getting the pat on the back she'd always wanted, and it felt odd but also oh-so-satisfying.

"Well, thanks. It's the least I could do."

"It's the *least* you can do?" Liz's eyebrow shot up, and her eyes squinted into scary slits.

"No, no," Hope stuttered. "I definitely do my best." She was shaken up and could feel her confidence cracking. "I was only joking."

"Hm…" Liz scribbled another note on the pad. "I don't remember hiring a comedian."

And with that, Hope's confidence shattered. Heat rushed to her cheeks and ears. A familiar feeling crept up from the pit of her stomach to her chest. She did her best to suppress it.

"With that being said. You're being reassigned." Liz continued.

"*Re*…assigned?"

Hope wasn't quite sure what she'd been assigned to in the first place. She wasn't on a team or part of any real projects. Her only job duty was wrangling unruly customers into submission via long, drawn-out, and often uncomfortable phone calls. Once they were taken care of, her co-workers could execute projects without a demanding client puffing their hot, overly demanding breath down their necks.

"Mr. Hensley met with all eight floor managers about "morale" and "employee happiness". Liz rolled her eyes and swatted her hand at her words like they were annoyingly buzzing in her face. "The result of that meeting was a restructuring of the company. And the result of restructuring is, apparently, new work for you".

"Wow. That's exciting. Thanks for the opportunity."

"Well, it's the *least* we could do." Her words dripped with sarcasm. Hope shrank into her chair and held back tears. Liz continued.

"You'll get a debriefing in your inbox by tomorrow morning. Nine O'clock. You'll have three business days after that before we expect results." She held up three long bony fingers for emphasis.

"*Three* days?"

"Is that a problem?"

"Oh. N-no...it's just so much time. That's all!"

"I see. Then you have two days." Liz scribbled another note before swiveling her chair around. "You can leave now."

As Hope returned to her cubicle, a swarm of emotions buzzed around her head, leaving her confused as to which feeling she should actually feel. After wrestling between embarrassment and anxiousness, she settled on hesitant optimism. The meeting went horribly, and she resolved to sulk about that later—maybe after dinner, but the new assignment seemed promising. After all, a new opportunity meant new ways to prove herself to be a valuable employee. She took a mental note to share the good news with Dr. Marley.

Hopefully, a restructuring includes opening the windows a smidge, Hope thought. Because of the lack of light, her typically deep brown skin was now more the color of lightly toasted bread, and she'd recently learned from her physician that she was vitamin D deficient.

♡♡♡

At the end of her workday, precisely at eight P.M., Hope quietly packed up her belongings—her cell phone, purse, and a granola bar she'd stuffed into her desk drawer as a midday snack. Then, she made her way to the nearest bus stop. She didn't have a car. Between paying rent, therapist fees, and student loans, she just couldn't afford one. She didn't mind her evening bus rides, though, as they gave her time to wind down and shut off her brain for the day. No corporate speak. No jargon. No watching her body language. When the bus arrived, she excitedly hopped on, sunk deep into the ripped leather seats, and sighed blissfully.

While waiting for the bus to start its journey, she looked up at her place of work. William Hensley and Associates. The most prestigious advertising agency in the South had a headquarters that was almost as impressive as its reputation. The massive glass building lit up at night, glowing purple, then green, then an ominous red, and back again. It was almost hypnotic.

The bus engine sputtered, pulling Hope out of her trance. As she rode, she watched the landscape morph from skyscraping office buildings and high-rises to small, compact condos and run-down apartment complexes. She was finally home.

♡♡♡

Hope lived in what was advertised as a "quaint one-bedroom condo in a charming neighborhood", which is a fancy way of saying "shit hole". Excuse the language, but sometimes only vulgarities will do.

The deep brown carpet wreaked of a mysterious odor she had yet to pinpoint, and the cream-colored paint slowly peeled from the walls, revealing the hideous chartreuse that was there before it. She could only imagine the kind of people who would paint their walls such a shocking shade of green, but they wouldn't have been friends of hers. Not that Hope had many friends to begin with, but she enjoyed the saying all the same. With all of its shortcomings, the absolute worst part of her living situation was the faulty plumbing. One toilet flush meant no running water for at least seven hours, leaving Hope with the unfortunate task of planning her showers around her bowels.

So yes, it was a shit hole. The only thing she liked about the place was her mahogany bookshelf, left behind by the previous owner. Whoever had occupied the space before her thought that chartreuse walls were acceptable, so it was no surprise they'd overlook such a beautiful piece of furniture.

The bookshelf was tall and sturdy, with intricate designs etched into its sides and across its top. Hope could tell it was made with the kind of gentle patience you'd only possess if you were in love. She imagined its creator had fallen head over heels for an avid book collector, and the bookshelf was his way of saying, "I'm madly in love with you. Stay with me forever". She must have accepted, placing her most prized possessions within his symbol of love. Now, the bookshelf housed *Hope's* most prized possessions. Her two-hundred-and-eighty book collection.

Hope plucked a faded orange book from the bookshelf and plopped down on her corduroy pull-out couch, which was also her bed.

One glance at the massive pile of dishes in her sink was enough to convince her that cooking could wait until the next day. Instead, she tore open a granola bar and nibbled on it, imagining it was something else. Something meatier. Like roast beef. Or chicken. She turned to chapter five of her orange book. The chapter heading read:

How To Be Likable.

This was becoming a habit of Hope's, as she would turn to this chapter whenever she had a particularly tough day at work. These kinds of days were becoming more and more prevalent. Of course, the work itself never really stressed her out. She hardly had any to do. Rather, it was the people that put her on edge. Hope's best friend Amber once explained that people were like books.

"You're supposed to read them and analyze what they say," she said. "But also read between the lines. Read the space around their words. Read their body language."

Hope would nod her head and say things like "That's true" and "You're right, Amber". But she was wrong. Books were comforting. They were an escape. And they were up to the reader's interpretation. People weren't like books, but Hope knew books could help her understand people.

The book she was currently reading was written by J.J. Martinez. The cover had long faded, but she remembered it started with a "D" or maybe it was a "B". Either way, the entire book was about starting your own business, something Hope wasn't too excited about. But chapter five? She needed chapter five.

Being likable is every person's desire, isn't it? We're all hungry to be loved, adored, and treated with respect. When people like you, they treat you with care, and, most importantly, they want to help you achieve success. While everyone wants to be likable, very few can do all it takes to be. And even fewer can keep it up. What can I say? People are fickle.

Hope nodded her head in agreement as she read. *People* are *fickle*, she thought. She continued reading, taking in his advice to be funnier, more charming, and dominating the conversation while also centering the other person. It wasn't until she reached page fifty-seven that she came across a line that made her pause.

Hope, you poor excuse of an adult. Spending your days prancing around pretending and spending your nights mending your sad, sullen ego. You probably haven't even done your dishes, have you?

She snapped the book shut. *Those words weren't there before.* She flipped back to page fifty-seven. The passage was gone. But it didn't matter. Whether the words were there or not, they rocked her to her core, and that's what bothered her the most. Hope shut the orange book and slid it back on the shelf.

Hope had suspected that her ability to "adult" wasn't on par with her peers, and she'd resolved to do better. While others were getting engaged and moving up in their companies, Hope stayed stuck. As her age climbed from twenty-three to twenty-four to her current age of twenty-five, the word "tomorrow" became increasingly prevalent in her vocabulary. She'd file her taxes tomorrow. She'd pay her rent tomorrow. She'd wash the dishes tomorrow. *No*, she thought, *I'll wash the dishes today. Right now. Right this instant.*

Hope hovered over her sink full of dishes, hoping to summon the will to wash them. To prove the words on page fifty-seven wrong. But after a few moments, she realized she didn't have a sponge, and she suddenly felt very childish.

"Wow, I am a crap adult, aren't I?" She sighed.

CHAPTER 2

— · —

THE ASSIGNMENT

"Absolutely, Mr. Johnson. Yes, yes, I definitely agree, it wasn't our best work..." Hope sat at her cubicle, twirling the phone cord as she whispered to the person on the other end. "The website? Yes, oh yes, it could definitely be better. You are absolutely right."

Mr. Johnson was one of the company's more troublesome clients, always calling to complain about one thing or the other. Hope had never met him in person but always imagined him to be a barrel-chested, older man with a sweaty upper lip. She zoned out as he continued to complain. She hadn't the faintest idea what he was yabbering on about, but considering his use of the words "doohickey" and "thingamajig" she was confident that he was in the dark himself.

"Uh-huh. Yes. You're right..." She checked the clock on her desk. It was eight-fifty-three. "Uh-huh. Ok, well, I'll tell you what. I'll send your complaint to the appropriate team right now and get it taken care of for you as soon as humanly possible. Sound good? Great. Have a nice day!"

As soon as she heard his answer of "And you as well!" she quickly hung up before he could sneak in any extra requests.

Just a few more minutes, she thought, shifting in her seat from the anticipation.

"Morning, Hope," Alex whispered before taking his seat, coffee mug in hand.

"Good morning," Hope answered dryly, keeping her eyes glued to the time on her clock. It was eight-fifty-five now.

"You feeling ok?"

Hope's ears perked up. She turned to face her cubicle neighbor, puzzled by his sudden interest in her life. Hope would've normally appreciated the friendly gesture, but the coffee incident was still fresh on her mind.

"I'm just fine. Thanks."

"That's good. I was worried." Alex smiled, then swiveled his chair around to face his computer.

Worried? To Hope, genuine worry was reserved for family and close friends, and Alex didn't fit under either one of those categories. She let his words of concern awkwardly float through the air before batting them away and turning to face her own computer. She woke it from its sleep, watching as its screen slowly brightened into a dull glow. At the bottom corner of the screen, a large red "one" bounced up and down like an unruly child begging for attention. It was nine o'clock.

Hope's mouse hovered over the notification, acknowledging her last few moments as a lowly Account Specialist. In only a few seconds, everything would change, and that book would be wrong. *That book.*

Hope shook the ominous feeling that crept up her chest and clicked the email:

Re-Assignment

Hey Hope,
It's Dale from floor six. Excited about
getting reassigned? You should be. Five
people from my floor were terminated, and
their work as a team has been given to you.
Exciting, right? Attached is a brief about
the Milton account and some, actually, a
ton of numbers for you to run and organize
into a 30-page report. We need to know what
we did wrong, what we did right, and what
you suggest we do moving forward. By next
Wednesday at 9 am sharp. Send the reports
to Liz.
  Don't let us down, Hope.
  Thanks, buddy.
  Dale.

Hope closed her eyes and reopened them to read the email
again. This time she wasn't imagining things. She really *was* given
the work of five people to complete in less than five days, if you
counted the weekend. She clicked the attachment and watched as
one-hundred-and-eighty-nine pages of information appeared on
her computer screen.

  Her foot began to nervously shake, which she quickly stifled.
She wanted to cry, to throw up her hands in frustration, but
instead, she thought of the pile of dishes in her sink. Those dishes

had been there since the Thursday before. That meant she'd gone eight days without cooking dinner.

"You're a poor excuse for an adult". The words of the book rolled through her brain, crashing into the sides of her skull and back again.

This is no way to live, she thought. She sat up straight and adjusted her glasses. There was no time to worry. It was time to be an adult.

♡♡♡

Hope decided the best way to tackle the project was to take things one step at a time. Unfortunately for her, the documents weren't labeled. Nor were they in any sort of order. At least none that made sense.

After a few hours of struggling to find clarity on her own, Hope knew she'd need to ask a few questions. This made her extremely nervous, as most things did. She feared appearing incompetent, but as she stared at the unlabeled pie charts and endless spreadsheets on the screen before her, she grew increasingly anxious. These weren't well-known facts or theories that she could research independently. This was the work of five people, and only those five people held the key to understanding. Those five people were also terminated.

Hope combed through each document, looking for any clues she could use, anything she could latch onto to help her solve the puzzle. She sifted and sifted, and on document number fifty-six she finally found something. It was a sales report, or maybe an inventory report, she couldn't quite tell, with hundreds of columns listing negative numbers next to positive numbers. No text, no dollar signs, and no indication of what it could be. Except for the document name. It was saved as "235xh_MacGregor_D.xls". D. MacGregor. That was a start.

Hope opened her email and responded to Dale from floor six:

```
Re:Re-Assignment

Hello Dale,
Thank you for sending these documents
over. The project is going well! But I
did need to chat with MacGregor about a
discrepancy in the report. Please send over
his email at your earliest convenience.
Thanks,
Hope
```

She pressed "send" and leaned back in her chair, proud of her ability to ask questions without really asking any questions.

Dale's response came seconds later and wasn't quite what she expected.

```
Re:Re:Re-Assignment

Hey there Hope,
Unfortunately, we're currently in a bit
of a legal tussle with MacGregor and the
other two on his team. Boring stuff. So,
I'm afraid I can't get you that email,
buddy. But I'm happy to hear the project is
```

```
going well. I'm sure one little discrepancy
won't affect your workflow too much.
  Rock on,
  Dale
```

Hope swallowed the lump in her throat, realizing that she'd not only *not* solved her problem but had dug herself deeper into the lie that she was competent.

As all fallen child prodigies eventually discover, once your age outpaces your talent, the "special" label that was firmly placed on you in your youth is ceremoniously ripped from your chest in an almost cruel manner.

Hope earned high marks all through school. In every class, her entire life. Until college, that is. She remembered the moment she tore open her report card to see a big fat "D" staring back at her. She wondered if she'd daydreamed too often during her professor's lectures. Maybe she'd spent too much time at the library laughing at her best friend's jokes. Or perhaps the boy in the blue baseball cap, the handsome one with the deep brown skin that sat two rows in front of her, had distracted her on test day.

Whatever the case, Hope's shining star had dimmed, and she cried, of course. But most importantly, she'd finally realized what others had accepted years before. She wasn't special. She didn't have any talents besides her intelligence, and now she knew that was a lie. And she decided to continue the lie. To perfect the act of perfection. To act as if she understood. To sit up straight and starch and iron her slacks until their sharp creases gave off the impression that her life was completely together.

It was that facade that had landed her the job at William Hensley & Associates. She'd breezed through her interview like it was old hat. Charming her then interviewer Bill, and easily making it through the three rounds thereafter. But it was during orientation that she was nearly exposed by Monica, who had asked her thoughts about the election. Hope stumbled, stuttering over her words, beads of sweat forming on her brow. She hadn't rehearsed politics. And Monica smirked, pleased with herself for chipping away at Hope's fortress of perfection.

Slowly but surely, Hope's true nature poked through. But she still held on by a thread, refining her act. Rather than stand out, she found it was easier to coast by. To fake, not perfection, but competency, and now even that was shattering before her.

After work, Hope rode bus line #6 back to her condo. Instead of her usual peaceful ride, Hope sat up straight and tense. Numbers and spreadsheets filled her mind, and for the first time ever, she'd taken her work home with her. As frustrated and exhausted as she was, this adult milestone had not gone unnoticed. She was oddly proud, although she hadn't accomplished much.

The bus came to a gentle halt at the stop about a block from her condo. Hope stood to make her departure, but before she could exit the bus, a hand lightly tapped her arm. It was the bus driver, Darius.

"Hard day at work?" he asked.

Darius only manned the bus on Wednesdays and Fridays. Still, he and Hope had established a friendly kind of relationship where they knew each other by name and wished each other a good night. Darius' strong build, defined jawline, and the raised scar above his eye led Hope to believe he was once a college athlete. Maybe even a star in his small hometown, but his dreams were dashed after an injury during the most pressing game of the season. Of course, it was just what she imagined. She could never bring herself to ask him anything about his past, just in case.

"Hm?"

"You usually sit right back there, all comfortable." Darius turned and pointed towards Hope's usual seat, his dreadlocks brushing against his muscular shoulder. "Now you're clutching that little briefcase, and you don't look comfortable at all."

Hope looked down at the leather briefcase in her hand. It was a graduation gift from her mother. It was in perfect condition because, until that week, she had never used it. There was no need.

"Listen," he continued, "I know you work for that big company. Are they treating you alright?" Darius gave Hope a look of deep concern.

"Oh, they're treating me fine." She smiled.

"You sure? Because my brother, he works for one of those companies. A huge one out West, and they...well, they make things really hard for him. Giving him too much work, or too little. Trying to sabotage him. Calling him names, then making him feel crazy for reporting them. You know what I mean?"

Hope knew exactly what Darius meant. "I do." Hope nodded. "I'm ok, though. Really. Just a little stressed."

"Well, ok. Hopefully, next time I see you on this bus, you're comfortable in that back seat again." He opened the doors. "Have a good night Ms. Hope."

"Hopefully. Good night, Darius." Hope stepped off the bus and onto the pavement. She walked past the run-down buildings and abandoned houses that paved the way to her abode.

On Hope's doorstep sat a package. She sucked her teeth in annoyance as she picked it up and tucked it under her left arm. The neighborhood had a problem with theft, and she'd informed the post office that it was to everyone's benefit to hold their packages. Instead, they continued dropping them off and leaving them as thief bait.

She plopped down on her couch-bed and examined the package. It was rectangular shaped and wrapped in deep purple paper. On the front, written in gold sharpie, were the words: *You'll be needing this.*

It must have been from Amber. Hope smiled as she carefully unwrapped the gift. She and Amber were as close as childhood friends, although they'd only just met in college. While Amber worked as a nurse in their midwest hometown, Hope moved down South to start work at William Hensley. The distance only deepened their friendship, as they'd regularly send surprise gifts to make up for it. Hope would send Amber mugs, keychains, and decorative cookies, but, to Hope's delight, Amber's gift was always the same—a book.

This time the hardcover was a deep burgundy with gold letters etched into it. There was no author, only a title that read: "How to be a Better Adult". Hope chuckled to herself. Amber knew this was just what she needed. She'd thank her later.

Hope slid the book onto her precious bookshelf, next to her faded orange book, and decided she'd give it a read as a treat after finishing the Milton Account. No time for fun and games when there was work to be done.

♡♡♡

Hope imagined that her peers cherished their weekends, using those two glorious days away from work to catch up with friends, spend time with family, or indulge in a drink or two. But when Hope wasn't entertaining fruitless suitors found while swiping on online dating profiles, she spent her weekends alone, curled up on her couch-bed with a good book. It had been a year since she moved from her small hometown to the hustle and bustle of the big city, and still, she felt like a stranger in a foreign land.

This particular weekend, Hope found herself scouring through documents, consuming gallons of the most caffeinated tea she could find, and forgetting to tend to her dishes.

By Sunday night, she was a full-fledged zombie dragging her feet and slurring her words. She'd barely made a dent in her work and struggled to stay awake and accomplish as much as possible. She took a sip of tea and moved on to the next document- #57. At the top of the page, it read:

Hope, you know you can't solve this. GIVE UP.

She squeezed her eyes shut and counted to ten before opening them again. The line was gone, instead replaced with "S.W.A.T. Analysis - Milton Account".

A small wave of panic washed over her, but only briefly. Sleep was drawing nearer, wrapping a pitch-black arm around her and slowly pulling her in deeper and deeper.

CHAPTER 3

THE LUNCH

On Monday morning, Hope frantically rushed through the front doors of the office with a single granola bar hanging from her mouth and, as she later found out when she was using the washroom after lunch, her fly unzipped. Before she could make it to the glass elevators and up to the third floor, she was greeted by Susan, the impossibly cheerful receptionist who sat perched at her desk, peering at Hope over her beakish nose. Her owlish eyes gleamed under the fluorescent lights.

"Morning, Hope!" she chirped.

"Good morning Susan!" Hope flashed her a smile, trying hard to control her heavy breathing—a result of darting from the bus stop. She'd been up all night working and lost track of time. Before she knew it, she was face down on her keyboard and had missed the first-morning bus.

"We're running a bit late this morning, aren't we?" Susan pointed to the clock on her desk. It was nine-fifteen. "We didn't think we'd see you today!"

Susan was one of those people who said "we" when they really meant "I". It was her gentle way of being a troublemaker. What she meant to say was, "You're late!! You're a bad girl, and I'm going to tell everyone!!!".

"Oh no," Hope replied with a forced smile, "You can't get rid of me *that* easily!"

The two laughed a bit *too* loud, then Hope made her way up to her cubicle, bracing herself for a scolding from Liz.

"Morning!" Alex flashed one of his million-dollar smiles as she walked past. "Sleep late?"

"Good morning." Hope smiled wide to shield the anxiety she felt bubbling in her chest. "Yeah, I had a pretty hard time sleeping last night."

"Ah, I see. Working hard, huh?"

Hope nodded. "Yep..."

"Well, I won't keep you, I know you've been busy." Alex swiveled to face his computer only to turn back around a few moments later. "Hey, so I heard about your new assignment..."

"You...did?"

"Yes, and I know it's a big one."

"Oh..."

"Do you know why they gave *you* that project?"

Hope shook her head no.

"It's strange. Isn't it? You'd think they'd assign it to someone more...seasoned."

"Well—" Hope didn't enjoy that Alex believed her to be "unseasoned", but she was more disturbed to be considered a topic of discussion in the office. "I can't say I find it strange."

"It's just that...well, I've been here longer than you. If anything, they should've given it to me. Not that I'm more capable, it just

makes sense. Doesn't it?" There was a slight crack in Alex's voice.
A difference from his usual confident persona.

Hope nodded her head. "I guess it makes sense."

"So, could you do me a favor, Hope? Could you let me help you
with that project? I know you've done a lot already, but I can pick
up the rest. What do you think?"

Hope racked her brain for the best way to say no. But as Alex
stared at her with his pleasant eyes and slight smile, what she said
instead was, "Ok, sure."

"Great! Let's go over it during lunch. I'll buy."

Hope nodded her head in agreement. She'd never interacted
with a co-worker outside of work, and even *at* work she'd
never moved beyond empty, whispered banter. She was suddenly
wrought with anxiety. *What if we run out of things to talk about?*
she thought, running through the mental catalog of conversation
starters she'd picked up over the years.

It was odd the way gossip spread through the office. After
phones were banned and Liz mandated the whisper policy, it
was nearly impossible to have a meaningful conversation without
either party whispering, "what did you say?" a dozen times.

So the floor relied on sticky notes to spread news—good,
bad, and unnecessary. No one stuck notes on Hope's desk, but
occasionally she'd find crumpled-up notes meant for Holly from
Janine in her wastebasket after lunch. One note described how
Janine had a one-night stand with a magician, who wooed her with
his tricks but ended up disappearing in thin air in the morning.
Hope wasn't quite sure whether the message was meant to be taken
literally. She never mentioned this because she was interested in the

juicy bits of conversation that had managed to flow her way and didn't want the accidents to stop.

As Hope trudged through the project, she couldn't help but wonder who could have possibly told Alex what she was working on. She ruled out Liz. She was too sensible to gossip and had she known work time was being devoted to discussing magical one-night stands, she would have found a way to nip that in the bud.

"You ready?" Alex had rolled his chair over to Hope's side of the cubicle.

Hope glanced at her clock. It was twelve o'clock on the dot. She nodded her head. "Yes, I'm ready."

"Great. Let's go! I'll drive."

"Drive?" Hope whispered. "But, we're not allowed to leave the building for lunch..."

"We sit here in the dark all day, we could use a little light. Don't you think?" He winked mischievously. "Come on."

Hope hesitantly followed Alex through the office to the glass elevators that sat at the other end of the floor. She could feel eyes in the dimness following the two as they maneuvered around the dark cubicles and glowing computer screens. She thought she might have even heard a gasp, but it could have been the stroke of computer keys or the groan of an old rolling chair.

As the two took the elevator down to the first floor, they filled the awkward atmosphere with the usual empty corporate banter. Crazy clients, swamped with work, tax time was right around the corner. By the time they reached the front desk, Hope worried that Alex would tell the others she was dull and not worthy of asking to lunch.

"See you in a few, Susan!" Alex waved at Susan, who sat perched at her desk like an owl, watching all of the comings and goings.

"Bye-bye, Alex!" She chirped before looking at Hope. "Oh wait. Are you two headed out...*together*?"

Hope rolled her eyes. In her head, of course. In reality, she gave her a weak smile.

"Yes, we're headed to that little cafe down the street for lunch. Cafe Dumont." Alex smiled wide as he spoke to her.

"So you're leaving the building for lunch? Isn't that against third-floor policy?" Susan leaned over the edge of her desk, eyes widened as if she had just heard a juicy secret.

"This is important business. Liz'll understand." Alex shot her a warm smile.

"Well, ok, if you say so." She slowly settled back onto her perch.

"See you after lunch, Susan. And hey, how about we bring you something? How does that sound?"

Susan's face lit up. "Sounds delicious!"

The two laughed together, and Alex waved goodbye. Hope remained quiet and held her breath as they left the building and walked towards the parking garage across the street. The sun bathed Hope in warm light. She squinted her eyes to shield her pupils from the intense rays. It wasn't often that she felt the sun, and she hadn't remembered it being so hot.

When the pair reached Alex's car, Hope was shocked by its sleek, high-end exterior. Alex caught her admiring eye.

"It was a gift." He opened the passenger door for her and waited for her to get in. "From my father."

"Well, he *definitely* loves you!" Hope said with a laugh as she settled into the comfortable leather seats. She was proud of herself. Her banter was improving.

A pained expression spread across Alex's face. "Yeah..."

Hope shrank a bit, realizing she may have made mistake. "Sorry."

"For what?" He sat in the driver's seat and paused. "You know, Hope, I owe you an apology."

"Me?"

"Yeah, for the other day. You're not my assistant. It's not your job to fetch me coffee. I was so deep into my work...I didn't realize what I was doing. But then Monica told me..." he glanced at his expensive-looking wristwatch. "Ah, we've got to get going."

He started the engine, and loud classical music blared from the speakers, drowning out the silence in the car.

What did Monica tell you?! Hope wanted to shout this, to shake Alex into finishing his statement. Instead, she turned to look out of the window and watched the landscapes blur by.

"Here we are."

Alex parked in front of a French corner cafe with an intricate carved wooden door framed by sprawling vines and blooming flowers. Outside, finely dressed patrons sat at round wrought iron tables and sipped out of fine china. Cafe Dumont looked like something out of a fairytale.

"Wow, it looks so nice!"

"Does it? That's a first." Alex chuckled and shoved his hands deep into his pockets. He walked past the cafe, turning the corner into an alley.

"A-Alex?" Hope hesitantly followed. "Alex?"

"Right here." Alex stood in the alley opening a small unmarked metal door and gesturing for Hope to enter. He must have caught the confused look on her face because he chuckled and added, "It's a hole in the wall."

"Hm, okay..."

Hope stepped through the door, and Alex crouched behind her, his tall frame a bit too lofty for the small entryway. A short set of steps led to a small dining room with two tables—one large and one small—and a cash register where an elderly woman was slumped over, sleeping and snoring quite loudly. On the walls was peeling floral wallpaper, almost as atrocious as the chartreuse that peeked from the walls of Hope's condo, and on the ceiling was a small crooked chandelier.

Alex tapped on the sleeping woman's shoulder, and she woke with a start.

"What? Where am I? Al? Al!" Her wide eyes were rimmed in cakey bright blue eyeshadow, and her frizzy white hair seemed to stand on end.

"Hey Nan, it's me, Alexander!"

"Oh, Alexander! My boy!" She gave Alex a warm embrace. "It's always good to see ya. And who is this beauty? A girlfriend, I hope." Nan winked. Alex laughed.

"No, this is my co-worker Hope. We don't have much time." He looked at his watch. "In fact, we should already be heading back to work—"

Hope gasped. She would surely get fired. She wondered if that was Alex's plan all along.

Alex continued, "—so we're gonna need our food fast."

"The usual?"

"The usual."

Nan disappeared through a set of double doors directly behind her, and Alex took a seat at the large table. "I've been coming here since I was a kid. I love this place."

"Shouldn't we be getting back to work?" Hope sat across from him.

"Don't worry, they won't fire you. Not today."

"What do you mean 'not today'?"

"We're both on the chopping block. But they won't swing the ax today. Not yet. Not so soon after the lawsuit." Alex removed a napkin from the dispenser on the table and laid it on his lap.

Panic shot through Hope's chest.

"Lawsuit? How do you know all this?" She remembered Dale's email. "Does this have to do with MacGregor?"

"Don't worry about the technicalities." Alex brushed away Hope's questions. "Just know that you don't deserve to be fired, and neither do I. So we've got to work together. Please, tell me about this project. What's the deal, and what can I do to help? If it gets done right, we'll both look good."

"Well—" Hope took a deep breath. Her foot nervously tapped against the shaky wooden table. "To be honest, I'm stuck. Most of the documents are unlabeled. There are spreadsheets with no values, pie charts with no numbers, and information with no meaning. I'm supposed to turn in a thirty-page report this Wednesday." She paused and looked down to suppress the tears of frustration that welled in her eyes. "I just don't know what to do."

At that moment, Nan burst through the door behind the cash register balancing two bowls of creamy escargot soup with baguettes. She hummed as she danced her way to the table, clinking the dishes down with a large toothy grin. Bits of soup flew out of the bowl and onto Hope's lap.

"Eat up!"

"Thanks, Nan!" Alex smiled and turned to Hope as he dipped his baguette into the broth. "You heard her. Eat up. It's good."

Hope did as she was told and spooned a tiny bit of soup into her mouth. While it was delicious, her worry robbed the taste from her tongue. *GIVE UP.* The words swirled through her thoughts, and this time they stuck.

"The project is impossible. Maybe, maybe we should just look for other jobs—"

Alex used his hand to bat away her idea. "I've been offered *three* other positions since last week, but I'm not accepting. Where's the challenge in that? I don't care about the job, they pay us peanuts, but I *do* care about coming out on top. I can't be fired. That's like...well, it's like *losing*."

"I suppose it is."

"So here's what we'll do. Don't worry about the project. I've got buddies who work with numbers. They owe me a favor or two. Just send me the documents, and by Wednesday morning, your problem will be solved. All I ask is to let Liz know I helped."

"I appreciate that, but I don't think this is meant to be a group project—"

"Hey, I'm sure they'd prefer it gets done, no matter the means. Don't you think?"

"Makes sense..." Hope thought about the offer. "So, if I do this, will I be one of those buddies who owes you a favor or two?"

A sly grin crept across Alex's face. "Of course."

♡♡♡

Back at the office, Alex tossed Susan a crepe from Cafe Dumont, which she caught with delight. Her nose pecked into the treat as she held it up to her face, taking in its sweet scent.

"Tell me if you love it, and I'll bring you more!" Alex winked, and Susan giggled like a schoolgirl.

"She'll keep her mouth shut now," Alex whispered in the elevator. Hope responded with an understanding nod.

She quite liked Alex. There was something about him, something she couldn't pinpoint, that made her want to spend more time with him. She was drawn to him. In fact, for the rest of the day, he was all she could think about.

CHAPTER 4

— ◆ —

THE BOOK

"Hey, Amber." After work, Hope spoke to her friend Amber on the phone. She worked nights at the hospital, so they usually only had one odd day a month to catch up. "How're things going with Jimoh?"

"Ugh, the usual! *Always* on the verge of packing up and leaving him."

"I'm sure he'll get it together soon." Jimoh was Amber's boyfriend of five years, and no matter how much she complained about him, Hope knew her friend was truly head-over-heels.

"Girl, forget him." Amber sucked her teeth. "How are things at work? You getting some sunlight?"

"No, still dim as ever, but everything's fine. I spent some time with a co-worker at lunch actually and, well—" Hope didn't want to worry her friend with threats of firing and overwhelming projects. "—how's the hospital?"

"Liz is letting you go to lunch now? Who was it? And the hospital's fine. Had another patient die on me last night. It gets less and less painful each time which worries me. I don't want to be desensitized by death, you know?"

"I'm sorry, I can't imagine how you feel. That must be the worse—"

"No, it's ok! Death is part of life, right? And it's my job. I knew what I signed up for." There were a few moments of silence on the other end. "Now, tell me about the co-worker."

"Well, he invited me to a French Cafe for lunch— "

"*He*? What's his name? Did he pay?"

"Alex, and yeah, he did."

"So you're finally embroiled in an office romance."

"No, it's not like that— "

"Of course it's like that, silly. A man doesn't pay unless he's interested."

"Well, maybe." Hope's mind was suddenly struck with a much more important thought. "Hey, Amber. Do you know what could be wrong with a person who's seeing things that aren't there?"

"Seeing things? Well, there could be a number of reasons for..." Her voice trailed, and Hope could hear muffled voices in the background.

"Amber?"

"Sorry, I've got to get to work." She returned to the phone with a hushed voice. "It was nice catching up as always."

"It was. And thanks for the book. It looks interesting."

"Book? I didn't send a book." Another pause. "Sorry, I have to go!"

The phone clicked, and Amber was gone.

Hope pulled the gift from her bookshelf. *Amber must be trying to trick me*, she thought before sitting on her couch-bed and opening *How to Be a Better Adult* to page one. There was no author, no publisher. Just a list. A bare-bones list that read:

1. Punch Fear In The Face

2. Dig Your Way Out Of Debt

3. Conquer The Workplace

4. Grab Life By The Horns

5. Chase Your Goals

6. Build Your Nest Egg

7. Seek 'The Ring'

8. Kiss Your Old Life Goodbye

Hope flipped through the rest of the book. There were hundreds of pages, and every single one besides the first was completely blank. Her suspicion was confirmed. It was a gag book. The ones they sell around April first to trick your bookish friends. It was a cruel joke, really, but not beyond Amber. In college, she was always the prankster. Hope sighed and slid the book into her briefcase. At least it would make a nice journal.

CHAPTER 5

— • —

THE SEVENTH FLOOR

The next morning, Alex didn't show up for work. This made Hope extremely uneasy. By noon, she had drafted an email asking about his whereabouts but then decided against it. If he had been fired, they would surely read any incoming emails of his. *But if he had been fired, she would surely be fired too.*

Hope knew her chances of completing the project before the next morning were slim. So she resigned to make the most of what she considered her last day at William Hensley & Associates. She printed out a few spreadsheets, readied her highlighter, and started work on a piece of art. She set out to create an intricate snail inspired by her lunch at Cafe Dumont.

As she finished up the snail's shell, a small red "one" appeared on her computer screen, grabbing her attention. It was an email from Monica requesting she come to her office on the seventh floor as soon as possible.

As a potential hire, a meeting with Monica meant you got the job. You'd meet with her for orientation and get a brief tour of all the best floors, then, at the end, you'd be released to your brand-new floor manager. It was exciting stuff. But for current employees, meetings with Monica were never a good thing. They either meant you were being reprimanded, fired, or encouraged to resign. And now, thanks to Alex, Hope knew she was on the chopping block.

"I'll be right up!" she responded before taking the elevator to the seventh floor.

The seventh floor was nothing like the third. It was bright and spacious, with no cubicles. Instead, groupings of tables took their place, lined with smiling employees that actually spoke to one another. Some were sharing screens, pointing, and explaining. Others leaned back in their chairs, laughing at what Hope was sure were witty office jokes. The glass offices that lined the back walls housed bean bag chairs and other colorful knick-knacks Hope couldn't quite make out, but she just knew they were fun. If Heaven were an office, the seventh floor would be it.

As Hope made her way to Monica's office, she locked eyes with Sarah Lynn, the seventh-floor manager, whose long blonde hair fluttered as she bent over laughing with a table of employees.

"Heya!" Sarah Lynn popped up and stuck her hand out for Hope to shake. "The name's Sarah Lynn, welcome to the seventh floor. Are you an intern? You must be an intern" She smiled wide, deepening the lines that framed her mouth.

Hope sighed. She'd met Sarah Lynn many times before.

"No, I'm Hope, remember? An Account Specialist from the third floor—"

"Aww, a new hire! A new hire? That's odd. Too bad you wound up on that gloomy third floor. But Liz is a doll! What do you need? Are you here for a tour? Of course, you're here for a tour..."

"No, I'm meeting with Monica—"

"Oh! You must be here for orientation. Of course." She crossed her arms and smiled deeply. "Follow me!"

Hope followed Sarah to Monica's office. The glass walls that made up her office were opaque, blurring her silhouette and shielding her from nosey co-workers.

"Here it is! Or is it?" Sarah Lynn laughed to herself. "Of course it is! Happy onboarding!"

Hope thanked her and knocked on the door.

"Come in!" A voice called out from within. Before Hope could reach for the knob, the door swung open, revealing Monica, who stood with a look that could only be interpreted as ire. "I said you could come in. Hurry, I don't have much time."

Hope entered and sat on one of the two leather chairs facing Monica's small desk. Monica took her place at the desk and weaved her fingers together. She gave Hope an accusatory look.

"You wanted to meet with me?" Hope asked while nervously adjusting her glasses.

"Yes," Monica rolled her eyes. "That's why I sent you a meeting request."

"Well, what's up?" Hope sighed.

"I hear your relationship with Alex has stepped into inappropriate territory."

"Wait, *what*?"

"You're allotted a twenty-minute lunch, and you were both gone for forty-three minutes yesterday." She tapped on her desk with her manicured finger, "I counted. What were you two doing?"

Hope clutched the arms of the chair, and her fingernails dug deep into the leather. "He invited me to lunch."

"And?"

"And that's it. We went to a cafe and came right back."

"See, that's the thing that puzzles me. First, you're fetching coffee for him like a lowly assistant, and now he's taking you to cafes. Something doesn't add up..."

"Alex asked me to go. Why aren't you asking him?"

"How do you know I haven't?" she snapped.

Hope remained silent, remembering Alex's absence.

Monica continued, "Have you heard about the budget cuts?"

Hope shook her head no.

"Well, now you know. Time is money, and people like you are expendable. Think about that next time you break the rules and go to lunch."

Hope thought of opposing and pressing Monica for what she meant by "people like you", but the pen in her hand caught her eye. That career-ending pen.

"I understand."

"Great! Have a productive day." Monica smiled and motioned towards the door.

♡♡♡

Hope did not have a productive day. She finished her snail art and moved on to a lopsided bear. Lopsided, because she was distracted. And she was worried about Alex.

She took one last look at Alex's empty chair before packing up for the day. She packed a little more than usual, as she figured she'd need a head-start when it came to clearing her desk after her inevitable firing. She wished that Monica had fired her right then and there. At least she would have gotten it over with.

Chapter 6

Punch Fear In The Face

Hope arrived for work an hour late. She hadn't gotten much sleep and instead stayed up sorting through all the possible outcomes of going to the office the next day. Would Liz give her a verbal lashing first before passing her on to Monica? Would Dale descend from the sixth floor to see her fumble in person? Or maybe Sarah Lynn would finally remember her name. It was a toss-up.

As Hope sidled past Susan's perch, she surprisingly didn't say a word. She only watched Hope with large, knowing eyes.

Hope trudged through the third-floor cubicle maze with her head down, avoiding the eyes that were surely following her movements. On that day, she appreciated the dimness, as it made it easier to disappear. Or at least try to.

She walked past Alex's empty chair and sat on her own, waking her computer from its deep slumber. There were messages waiting for her, of course. Two, to be exact. One was a message from Liz, and the other an urgent email from Dale. Hope's shaky hand hovered her mouse over the urgent message before opening it:

`Re:Re:Re:Re-Assignment`

```
Hi Hope,
Great job on the project. Alex sent it
over. You two make a stand-up team. Look
out for a follow-up meeting with Liz.
Stay groovy,
Dale
```

She breathed a sigh of relief and stifled the smile that fought to creep across her face. So Alex still kept his word. Hope happily moved on to Liz's email, expecting a message of congratulations, the same a war hero would receive after returning home, bruised and battered but still victorious. Instead, the message only contained three words: "My office. 1pm."

When the time came for Hope's meeting with Liz, she never expected to see Monica sitting beside Liz with an eerily smug look on her face. She had never expected that as she sat on the tiny chair that was dwarfed by Liz's tall alabaster desk, she would say the words: "We need to discuss your termination."

It was almost like a dream after that. Or rather, a nightmare. Hope tuned out the words, only hearing the hollow click of Liz's talons tapping on her desk. She watched as Monica's tongue whipped out of her mouth, licking her teeth like a serpent. And her venomous eyes watched Hope with glee. A familiar feeling of dread crept from Hope's belly into her chest, then her throat, nearly suffocating her.

"The Handbook says three strikes before you're fired. And according to Monica, you have broken the rules now three times." Liz held up three bony fingers, one by one.

"You took a forty-minute lunch, I counted," Monica interjected, a wide smile on her face. "And you were an hour late this morning—"

"And most importantly..." Liz shot Monica an icy look, regaining control of the conversation. Monica recoiled. "You handed off confidential files to another employee."

"Yes, b-but the project. It was completed. Isn't that what matters?" Hope snapped out of the haze to defend herself.

"No. What matters is we've lost faith in you, Hope. Please remove your belongings from your desk and don't come back tomorrow."

The thought of bills, loans, and payments rushed into the forefront of Hope's mind. You see, when faced with a threat to survival, it is the instinct of the Homosapien to either fight, freeze, or flee. Hope's normal frequency was set to freeze. She would process the unpleasantries later and remain stiff and stoic in the moment. Maybe even flash a smile because, you know, no hard feelings. At least none that were safe to express. But this time, she chose to fight.

"But this isn't fair. I was never informed that the project was confidential. I've followed your insane rules for over a year. What's really going on here?"

Liz paused her tapping, and Monica shifted in her seat.

"What's going on here..." said Liz. "...is the fact that you're fired, and you need to leave immediately. You broke the rules. Simple as that."

♡♡♡

Hope stormed out of Liz's office in a gloriously dramatic fashion. She shot out of her chair, knocking it over, then slammed

Liz's office door on her way out. Had she been a stage actress, she would have surely won an award for her impassioned performance. Her hunched-over co-workers looked up in unison, watching her as she flew through the office and into the hallway.

Hope continued on, walking briskly down the end of the hall, briefcase in hand, occasionally adjusting her glasses and checking her watch to give off the impression that she had somewhere urgent to be. She turned the corner, making sure she was out of sight, and quickly slid into the unisex bathroom.

She locked the door behind her, sat in a corner across from the toilet, and pulled her knees up to her chest. Was it gross? Yes, definitely, but her mind was too preoccupied to acknowledge that she was curled up on the mildly moist floor of a public bathroom. Instead, it told her she was incompetent, small, and worthless. She laid her head down in her arms and released a shower of tears. She had to remind herself to breathe in between the heaving and sobbing that rocked her entire body. She felt her eyes swell with the weight of the sorrow that kept her anchored to the floor. Her tears dampened her impeccably pressed blouse, but she didn't care. That's a lie. She did care, very much so. It was her favorite blouse. But she cried anyway until the unbearable weight that she felt in her chest slowly lifted, leaving behind an empty, gaping hole of nothingness.

Hope had no idea how long she'd been in the bathroom. After her tears ran out, she sat on the tiled floor, letting the waves of nothingness wash over her. She didn't want to see anyone. She didn't want to go anywhere. She had no motivation to do anything. So she sat.

There was a knock on the door. She didn't answer but watched as the door handle jiggled.

"Hello? Is someone in there?" A male voice called through the door.

She wanted so badly to answer. The words vibrated in her vocal cords, but her lips remained sealed, and nothing came out.

The man groaned, and she heard his heavy footsteps become fainter and fainter. He must have thrown his hands up in frustration before stomping down the hall to the larger multi-stalled restroom.

More time passed before Hope decided to move, choosing to reach for her briefcase. When she had similar episodes in the past, the only thing that helped her was writing in her journal, and luckily, she remembered she had a journal right there in the stall with her.

She unzipped the leather briefcase and pulled out *How to Be a Better Adult*. She slid a fresh new pen from the inner pocket of her bag. After taking a deep, wavering breath, Hope opened the book to page two. The blank page was no longer blank, and this time she wasn't surprised to see words where they weren't before:

PUNCH FEAR IN THE FACE

You're terrified, aren't you? You're not alone. Everyone is terrified. Adulthood is like walking on a tightrope, and you're getting shakier, but you're too far across to turn back. It's full of work. Hard work. Sometimes unfair work. Mostly unfair work. And the possibility of failure lingers with each passing day. You could be fired at any moment, for any reason. Someone could steal your identity and run your credit into the ground. A willowy woman could saunter by, attract your husband's wandering eye and wreck your ten-year marriage. It's all so very scary.

The scary parts won't ever go away. So what needs to change is you. You need to square up and punch Fear in the face. Right between the eyes. And once you've faced the Fear head-on, you'll be able to move forward in spite of it.

ACTION ITEM: *Punch Fear in the face.*

It felt as if the writer had crawled into Hope's brain and made a nice, comfortable home for herself. Every word resonated with her and wrapped her in a comforting embrace. She turned to the next page, hungry for more, but the rest was still blank.

Rather than wallow in disappointment, Hope wiped her eyes and stood to look at herself in the mirror. She was flushed and pale, and her eyes were rimmed in black—a product of her smeared mascara. She used to invest in waterproof makeup for this very reason, but she hadn't had a proper panic attack since college, so she decided to stick with the cheap stuff.

Just like in college, she did what she could to salvage her appearance. She cleaned her glasses with a corner of her blouse. She wet a few squares of toilet tissue and wiped away her makeup. she splashed some cold water on her face and patted it dry. She took off her blouse and slacks and dried them for a few minutes under the hand dryer. They ended up with even more wrinkles than they started with, but at least they were dry. She put them back on and reevaluated herself. With her bare face and pale skin, she could pass as sick, and maybe if she coughed and sniffled a bit people would think she only had a cold.

Hope packed her precious book back into her briefcase and quietly slid out of the bathroom. She turned the corner and walked down the hallway towards the elevators. The thought of returning to her desk to collect the rest of her items crossed her mind, but there was nothing there that she needed. The laptop belonged to the company, after all, and they could keep the granola bars.

On the first floor, Hope shuffled past Susan, avoiding eye contact once more.

"Leaving?" Susan chirped while her large eyes gleamed in the light.

"Yes," Hope turned to face the owly-eyed woman. "I'm sick."

"Oh, really?" She smirked. "Hm. Feel better." Her words dripped with insincerity.

Hope left her now former place of work and waited at the bus stop for Line #6 to make its way back around to pick her up. She checked her watch, it'd be another fifteen minutes. She settled onto the bench, unzipped her briefcase, and pulled out *How to Be a Better Adult*, opening it to where she last left off. She reread the last tip: "Punch Fear in the face."

Hope thought it odd how the word "Fear" was capitalized, giving it a sort of living, breathing quality. She imagined fear as a hulking eight-legged creature with long pointed fangs salivating at the mouth as it ravenously devoured the dreams of anyone it crossed paths with. *How can I fight that*, she thought.

The bus arrived three minutes late, and when the doors swung open, Hope was face to face with Darius, who was visibly surprised to see her.

"Hope? I'm surprised to see you at this time." He examined her flushed face as she stepped onto the bus. "You ok?"

Hope sat in the seat behind Darius, looking up to find his eyes watching her in the rearview mirror.

"I'm fine. Everything is ok." Hope's voice trembled as she spoke. She closed her eyes, and tears began to well behind her lids.

"You don't seem alright. Now, if someone at that company is bothering you—"

"I've been fired." Hope blurted out, keeping her eyes squeezed shut.

Darius didn't say a word in response. Instead, he checked the watch on his wrist and turned the keys in the ignition. The bus engine growled as it began to slowly roll off, joining the lunchtime traffic. As the bus rolled along, Hope could feel every turn, every bump, every stop. After some time, she opened her eyes and looked out of the bus windows. The landscape was unfamiliar, and the towering buildings that made up the business district were now replaced with rectangular two-story houses settled behind freshly mowed lawns with square, neatly trimmed bushes. Line #6 was not on its usual route.

Hope sat up straight in her seat. "Where are we?"

Darius glanced at her in the rearview mirror. "We're where we need to be. We take a different route in the afternoons."

"I see."

They rode in silence for a few moments before Darius spoke again.

"Hey, Hope. Did I ever tell you about my accident?" He pointed to the scar above his eye.

Hope shifted uncomfortably. She almost didn't want to know because afterward, she'd have to express the appropriate response, and she was never the best at consoling.

"No, you haven't..."

"Ah, well, I suppose I don't discuss it much. I know people wonder, though..." His eyes briefly met Hope's in the rearview mirror before returning to the road. "Before I became the man you see today, I was a professional boxer. Yup, I was. The Kid Wonder is what they called me because I was so young. Only fourteen taking down guys twice my age, can you believe it? And I won every match. Every single one. No one could touch me." Darius paused for a moment to make a left turn before resuming.

"I was in the game for seven years before the pain set in. With every fight, my body took a real beating. But I was young, and I healed fast. Until I wasn't that young anymore. When I turned twenty-one, I turned to drinking. It was the only way to not feel, you know? I'd drink until I couldn't see anymore. And then I'd drive." He rolled to a stop at a red light.

"And one day, I drove me and my cousin into a ditch. I don't remember any of it. But when I woke up in the hospital, my cousin was in jail. Drunk driving. Guess he switched spots with me when I passed out and climbed into the driver's seat. He told me I was young, that I had my whole career ahead of me." The light turned green, and the bus rolled on.

"But he didn't know I was so badly injured. They told me I could never fight professionally again. Something about my muscles. I don't know. Didn't matter at that point. I thought my life was over. Kind of like how you're feeling right about now." He stole another glance in the mirror.

"But you know what? It's been ten long years since then, and I've been training again. Building up muscle. Haven't touched a drink in years, even though I'm still in pain. But I'm determined to prove something. I'm going back in the ring next week, and something is telling me that you should be there to see it."

"I'd love to come. Where is it?"

"It's at the Carbon Theatre. Sunday night at nine."

"I'll be there." Hope smiled.

The bus came to a stop a block away from Hope's condo. When she stood to make her exit, Darius turned and smiled wide.

"Can you guess who I'm fighting first?" He punched the air in front of him, pretending to spar with an imaginary opponent.

"Who?"

"The Fear."

Hope was convinced she was hearing things. She shook her head and asked, "Excuse me?"

"I know it's a long shot, believe me," Darius laughed. "No one beats Victor "The Fear" Sanchez, but I've got a good feeling about this one. I do."

"Punch Fear in the face." Hope repeated the words she had read in the book.

"That's the plan. Right between the eyes." Darius pulled a business card from his breast pocket and handed it to Hope. The photo on the front was of a younger him.

"This has all my contact information. Hope to see you there, Ms. Hope."

"I definitely will be there. Thanks for the invite." Hope took the card and stepped off the bus and onto the pavement.

As she walked past the decrepit apartment complexes and dead grass that made up her neighborhood, she thought long and hard about Darius and his determination to fight again. She crossed the street toward an abandoned house, letting her hand trace the wired fence that surrounded it.

Darius could have just gone about his life, driving his bus and going home to whatever awaited him there. Nothing wrong with that. But still, he wanted more. And so did Hope. She walked past her condo, turned right, and continued walking three blocks East toward the public library. She had a mission now. She had to learn everything there was to know about Victor Sanchez. She had found her Fear.

CHAPTER 7

THE LIBRARY

Hope was never a fan of reading borrowed books. To her, books carried more than the stories inside of them. They carried memories with each page. Hope found it eerie when she would flip through pages and see someone else's notes or nicks from when someone else dropped the book. It was like seeing the traces of ghosts, and it always rubbed her the wrong way. And for that reason, Hope steered clear of libraries. But now she had a mission worthy enough to break her library ban. And, thanks to her firing, she didn't own a laptop anymore.

Hope pulled open the library doors expecting to be greeted by hushed silence and the cold stare of a librarian, but instead, as she stepped through the entrance, she was surprised to see a tiny table with a brown flag perched next to it, covered in bright pink painted handprints. Behind the table stood three little girls, no older than thirteen but no younger than seven. They each wore knee-high socks, cuffed khaki shorts, and yellow t-shirts with pink letters that read "Blossom Scouts Troop #570".

"Hello, Miss." A tall, lanky teen with short, kinky hair spoke first. She puffed up her chest and held up a clipboard. "Name's Sofia, and this is Lindsey and Tasha. We're your local Blossom

Scouts. Well, not really local. We're from the next town over. But we're selling cookies to raise money for our camping trip to Bird Lake."

"Going to Bird Lake would be a dream come true!" The smallest girl, Tasha, chirped excitedly while holding up a box of cookies. Her beaded braids clattered as she jumped up and down.

Lindsey, a freckled, bespectacled young girl, gently jabbed Tasha's arm with her elbow, signaling for her to hush. Tasha settled down and stood, chest up, mimicking Sofia's pose.

Sofia continued, unfazed by the interruption.

"Would you consider buying a dozen cookies or making a small donation?" She pinched her fingers together as she said the word small. For emphasis.

Hope had been forced into fundraising before. When her mother enrolled her in an after-school club at church, she was sent door to door in a fairy princess costume, asking strangers to donate and "keep the magic alive". The donations were never enough, and Hope's magic withered away and died. Because of these fading memories, Hope was usually inclined to donate, but in this particular moment, she didn't think it wise since she had just been fired.

She stooped down to the girls' level like a patient teacher and whispered, "I'm sorry. I don't have any cash."

The two smallest scouts hung their heads in disappointment.

"It's ok, miss. We take all major debit cards." Sofia tapped on a line on her clipboard with a pen.

"I'm sorry I forgot my cards at home." Hope was taken aback by the young girl's determination.

"Check?"

"I-I don't have a checkbook."

"Well, that's alright, miss." The girl saluted, and the younger girls followed. "Have a nice day!"

Hope smiled and hurriedly walked away, still reeling from the pressure, and made her way to the computer room near the back of the library. The computers were much older than the ones at work, and waking them up was much more difficult. Hope clicked her mouse and tapped on her keyboard until, finally, the computer screen came to life.

Now impatient, Hope opened a browser and typed: "Victor "The Fear" Sanchez". Pages and pages of articles appeared with titles that read: "Facing the Fear? Good Luck!" and "Sanchez Wins Again! Watch Him Pummel His Opponent to a Pulp". She combed through news updates and fighter profiles to learn everything she could about the boxer.

He was six-foot-three, had an eighty-two-inch reach, and an unorthodox fighting style. He was right-handed with a strong left jab. And, most importantly, he was undefeated. Forty-four to zero. Hope gulped. She had a lot of work to do in the next four days.

"Library's closing."

Hope looked up from a thick book of boxer training techniques to see a security guard hovering above her. She checked her watch. It was seven o'clock.

"Oh wow, I must have lost track of time, sorry."

The security guard grunted and continued making his rounds. Hope placed the book back on the shelf she had found it, and made the journey back to her condo.

"Stay out of the danger zone", she recited to herself as she walked, remembering a technique from a book. "Never stop moving. Attack the body."

Normally on a night like this, she would have wallowed in her own self-pity, replaying the day's events over and over again in her mind like a sick rerun of a particularly frightening horror movie. But as she settled into her couch-bed for the night, all she could think about was fighting The Fear.

CHAPTER 8

— · —

THE PARK

The next morning Hope arose bright and early. She had a plan and she couldn't afford to waste the day cooped up inside. She stretched and crept to the bathroom, where she ran a pick through her hair, brushed her teeth, used the toilet, flushed the toilet, and—she had forgotten about the unfortunate plumbing situation. But not until after she stood in the shower naked and ready to hose off the disappointment of the day before. She turned the handle from off to hot, and nothing came out. Not even a drop. She sighed with defeat and wrapped herself in a robe.

On any other Thursday, she would have ironed her slacks, slid on a plain white blouse, and pulled her hair up into a tight bun. But on this particular Thursday, she braided her hair down into two neat plaits, dug out her only pair of jogging pants, and slid her feet into her only pair of sneakers. She'd had them since high school.

Hope carried her briefcase to the bus stop. She knew it was an odd sight, but the briefcase housed her book, and she couldn't leave her house without it. The bus arrived, coming to a gentle stop before her. For a brief moment, when the doors opened, she had hoped she would see Darius in the driver's seat. But instead, a tall man with a tiny mustache and beard sat in his place.

"Good morning." The driver said with a smile as Hope sidled on.

"Good morning." Hope dropped her change into the box next to him, picked up a map, and took her seat. She looked over the map to make sure she was heading in the right direction.

"Where ya headed?" The driver watched her in the rearview mirror, just like Darius.

"Green Acre Park. Near ninth street."

"Don't worry about that map, ma'am. I'll let you know when it's time to get off."

Hope smiled and thanked the man.

At the park, Hope took in her surroundings. She'd only been once before when she had first moved to the city, but plenty had changed since then. The trees were taller, greener, and lusher. The bushes were neatly trimmed, and the cars in the parking lot were much fancier than she'd remembered. Even the playground was different. The old swing set that used to creak and groan as children swung and swayed on it was replaced by an art installation—a giant colorful koi fish with a gaping mouth. Its painted metal body twisted up towards the sky, and a bronze plaque rested at its tail fin. The old rusty slide was also gone. Instead, a sprawling fountain took its place, with young children gathered around it, splashing or tossing coins into its watery belly. Hope walked past the new additions to the one thing that hadn't changed a bit—the walking path.

The path circled and looped around the park and was peppered with rudimentary exercise equipment. There were bars and hoops and other copper contraptions people used before there was such a thing as electricity.

Hope had never been the most active person. In fact, she never exercised. Not that she didn't want to. It's just that books held precedence, and she couldn't put one down long enough to find the time.

But, of course, that day was different. Briefcase in hand, she jogged through the park, her mind fully fixated on fighting The Fear. She had to get stronger, much stronger, but most importantly, she had to get faster. Her tiny feet thumped against the dirt path in a quickening but steady rhythm. She imagined herself bobbing and weaving her way around the Fear's massive build and gangly arms. She gracefully sidestepped, evading his powerful blows, before ducking, winding up her arm, and slicing the air with her closed fist as she dealt him a crushing blow to the jaw.

She smirked to herself. Soon, her dream would become a reality.

Hope slowed as she spotted her first stop on the path. They were monkey bars that had once been multicolored but had since rusted brown with time. Hope laid her briefcase at the base of the bars and grabbed the first bar, lifting her feet from the ground. As she made her way from one bar to the next, she heard a rustling directly behind her. She hopped down and turned to investigate the noise. There was nothing around but the bushes and trees that framed the path.

"Hello?" she asked to no one.

In the distance, she could hear the high-pitched coos and laughter of young children splashing around the fountain or playing tag around the koi fish.

"Hello?" she asked again, a bit louder. She heard low murmuring and crept towards the sound, slowly parting the greenery with her hand. As she pushed away leaves and branches, she braced herself for what could be hiding. What she revealed was nothing. She shrugged, placing blame on the wind before turning to continue her jog. She reached for her briefcase, eager to feel the soft leather of the handle against her fingertips and the weight of her precious book safely encased within it. Instead, her fingers hit dirt. Her briefcase was gone.

Hope frantically glanced about. *Maybe I simply kicked it over,* she thought, pushing away leaves and branches around the area. More rustling. Hope whipped around and caught sight of a little shoe darting deep into the greenery.

"Hey!" Hope tried following the little shoe, which was attached to a little body donned in overalls, dashing through the bushes and trees back towards the park, but she became entangled in the branches, with leaves blinding her as she ran through.

"Come back here!" she yelled, her voice cracking.

She finally burst through the leaves to see a child, a boy, running back towards the park, her briefcase gripped by his tiny hand. Her heartbeat quickened as she kicked up her heels and sped to catch the rapscallion.

"Hey!" she yelled, attracting the attention of the mothers in the park, who all turned and looked on in horror as Hope chased the young boy.

He giggled and looked over his shoulder at Hope. His two front teeth were missing, leaving a mischievous gap, and his jet-black hair blew straight back in the wind.

"What exactly is going on here?" As the pair reached the statue, a tall, glamorous woman stepped in front of Hope with arms crossed, pausing her chase.

Her straight dark hair matched that of the boy's, and so did her face in a way, but with all of her teeth accounted for. She wore a pink tweed jacket, and a pair of designer cat eye sunglasses sat atop her head. On her finger, a massive diamond ring glinted in the sunlight. "Why are you chasing my son?"

Hope stopped to catch her breath.

"He...he took...he took my briefcase." Hope pointed at the child, who hid behind the thin woman's legs, embracing them with a wide gaping smile still plastered on his face.

"Ki-woo." The woman looked down at the boy. "Is it true you took this woman's briefcase?"

"No, mommy." The smile left Ki-woo's face as he shook his head no, clutching the briefcase against his chest.

"Well, there you go." She looked back at Hope. "He didn't take your briefcase."

"But ma'am—" Hope's jaw dropped in disbelief.

The woman held up her hand and said, "It's Donna."

"Sorry, Donna—

"But *you* can call me Mrs. Choi."

"But, Mrs. Choi." Hope inhaled deeply. "He's holding it. Right there in his arms. Don't you see it?"

"If my son says he didn't take it, then he didn't take it. Are you calling my Ki-woo a thief?"

"No, but I understand that children tend to...*grab* things that may not be theirs. I don't want to trouble you. I'm just in need of my bag—" Hope bent over and reached for the bag.

Ki-woo swiveled his small body around.

"Mine!" he whimpered. Tears began to well in his eyes. "It's mine. My bag. I love it."

"I suggest you leave my son and his bag alone."

"If it's his bag, then why is my name etched inside?" Hope scoffed.

Ki-woo stopped whimpering, opened the bag, and gasped, then held it up, showing the inside to his mother.

"What does it say?" he asked.

"Let's see, dear. It says 'Hope Oh-bee-acko'. Well, what do you know?"

"It's Oh-bee-awko." Hope snapped before bending on one knee, bringing herself to eye level with the young boy. "That's me," she cooed, reaching her hand out to accept the bag.

Ki-woo burst into tears as he placed the bag in Hope's hand. Mrs. Choi looked down at him nervously, awkwardly patting him on the head.

"There, there?" The boy cried even louder, rocking Hope's eardrums. Mrs. Choi sighed and slid her sunglasses onto her face, shielding her eyes. "You're embarrassing us Ki-woo."

Hope's annoyance softened into pity as she watched the struggling mother pick up the flailing child. When Mrs. Choi spoke next, her voice was strained and sharp.

"Ok, it's yours. Fine. I'll buy the bag from you. How much?" she asked, pulling her wallet from her dainty side bag and opening the clasp.

"Well, uh." Hope hesitated. Maybe this was fate. The woman obviously had more money than Hope had probably seen in a lifetime. But something tugged at her, telling her not to accept. It was her conscience, maybe. "It's ok. It's his, free. I just need what's inside."

Hope pulled her beloved book from the bag and a pen for notes, then handed it over to the weeping boy, who snatched it from her hands without saying a word. His wails turned into whimpers, and his gaping smile slowly returned to his face.

"Where's the receipt?" asked Mrs. Choi.

"Mine!" declared Ki-woo.

"That's right. It's yours. It's all yours. No more crying, ok?" Mrs. Choi bounced Ki-woo on her hip.

Ki-woo simply responded with a giggle.

Hope blinked. "A receipt?"

"I need a receipt for every transaction. For my records. Don't you know anything about taxes?"

"Ah. Right." Hope had forgotten about her taxes.

She dug through her pockets to find a scrap of paper. Whatever had been written on it previously had since faded. She scribbled "zero dollars, for leather briefcase" then took note of the date and signed it, before handing it to an impatient-looking Mrs. Choi.

"Thank you, Ms. 'Oh-Bee-Awko'. Nice doing business with you."

Mrs. Choi slid the receipt into her wallet and snapped it shut. Before Hope could thank her for her business, she turned and briskly strutted off towards the parked cars in the lot across the park, with Ki-woo still balancing on her hip.

Hope clutched her book to her chest, embracing it like a long-lost friend. *That was a close one*, she thought. She decided that in order to be a successful adult, not only did she have to punch fear in the face but also stay far, far away from children.

♡♡♡

In the days that followed, Hope continued her morning workout routine. She'd wake up early, plait her hair, and go for a run around her neighborhood. In the afternoons, at home, she'd continue with push-ups and sit-ups. In the evening, she spent hours at the library reading about famous boxers and their legendary techniques.

By the time Sunday rolled around, she was ready. Not physically, of course, but she *felt* ready, and that's all that mattered to her. The Fear didn't stand a chance.

Chapter 9

The Fight

Sunday night found Hope seated at the packed Carbon Theater, surrounded by unruly boxing fans. The bright lights above the ring pierced through the darkness of the arena, and the crowd's chattering and seat shifting grew into one massive thunder of a sound.

The announcer, donning a crisp black suit, stood in the center of the ring as each man took their place on either end, readying to fight.

"The first on my right, fighting out of the red corner, wearing black trunks with green trim." The announcer spoke into his microphone that hung from the heavens. "He weighs in at two-hundred-and-thirty-four pounds. His record stands at thirty wins and zero losses. Known as the Slick Mouth of the South and formerly The Kid Wonder, please welcome former heavyweight boxing champion Dariusssss Smithhhhh!"

The crowd cheered as Darius' manager removed the black robe that had been draped over his hulking body. Darius hopped from side to side, flexing his muscles and glaring at his opponent.

The announcer continued.

"And on my left, fighting out of the blue corner, wearing red trunks with gold trim, weighing in at a massive two hundred and seventy-nine pounds," he paused as the crowd went wild, continuing only after they had quieted down. "His record stands at forty-four wins and zero losses. He's known as the Big Mean Knock Out King and The Fear. Please welcome the heavyweight champion of the world—the one and only Victooooor Sannnchez."

The hood that shrouded Victor's face in darkness was removed by his handlers, revealing his deep brown skin and tightly curled hair. Despite being known as The Fear, his eyes were soft and friendly. He smiled at Darius as his tall body bobbed from side to side.

The announcer stepped aside, allowing a small mousy man to shuffle to the center of the ring, summoning both men to join him. Mic in hand, bowtie strapped tightly around his neck, and sweat stains seeping from under his arms, the man spoke, listing off various rules that Hope couldn't quite understand through his thick Australian accent. At the end of his speech, both men tapped gloves and returned to their assigned corners.

A bell rang, and the men lurched towards each other, their bodies bobbing and swaying like two buoys floating together in the ocean. As one stepped back, the other would lunge forward, jabbing gently. For a moment, it almost felt rehearsed. Hope imagined them lacing up their dancing shoes backstage to run through the routine "just one more time".

In mere seconds their lunges quickened, and their punches became more powerful and increasingly accurate. Darius fought furiously, hammering his fists into The Fear's body, leaving him backed against the ropes, covering his face with his gloves. A moment later, The Fear ducked and dashed around Darius, showering him with a hailstorm of punches. Darius became disoriented, falling back onto the ropes.

Before he could catch his bearings, The Fear swung again and again, his long arms whipping through the air like ropes. Darius stumbled forward, grabbing his waist like Ki-woo had embraced his mother's legs, and The Fear whipped around, slamming him to the ground with a thud. The crowd cheered as Darius shakily stood to his feet. A pained expression spread across his face. Hope nervously pulled at a loose thread in her jeans. She wanted so badly to look away but couldn't.

The fight wore on, with both men taking turns swinging and ducking. Their breathing became heavier, and their movements slowed. By the third round, Darius had a permanent scowl on his face. His legs shook a bit. He had been punched in the face quite a few times, and the flesh above his left eye was swollen.

Darius staggered as he swung, aiming for the Fear's face. The Fear ducked, leaving Darius' side exposed. In an instant, The Fear's fist flew through the air, landing squarely in his ribs. Darius stumbled and fell to his knees as if in deep prayer. The tiny, bowtied man sidled beside him and began counting to ten with his fingers as the Fear stood over Darius, the smile returning to his face.

Hope sat at the edge of her seat, willing Darius to stand. No matter how shaky, she wanted him to fight to his feet and continue. But as the count reached eight, then nine, then ten, Darius remained still, and the Fear was victorious. Hope's heart sank to the pit of her stomach as she watched the tiny man lift The Fear's arm in the air, a sign of victory. The crowd wildly cheered, standing to their feet and pounding on the bleachers like animals. The Fear marched around the ring, both hands in the air as Darius crumpled into a tiny ball on the ring floor, his manager hobbling over to him and patting him on the back. He winced and beat his fist on the ground.

While the people around her stood and cheered, Hope remained seated as heat rose to her cheeks and tears welled in her eyes. Darius' loss was her loss, and she felt his pain deeply. And then she felt rage. *It's not fair*, she thought, *It's just not fair*.

Hope shot to her feet, climbed down from the bleachers, and stormed towards the ring. She breezed past a security guard who grabbed at her sweater, shouting, "Ma'am! Ma'am?". But she wriggled free and continued on, climbing into the ring as the security guard chased closely behind, nipping at her heels like a hound.

As she scrambled to her feet, the crowd's cheers fell to a hushed murmur.

Darius' eyes widened. "Hope, what are you doing?" He tried to stand but winced and fell back onto his stool.

The Fear turned to face her, his eyes full of amusement and a smirk plastered on his face. "What's going on here? Fan meet and greets are after the show."

"I'm not a fan." Hope stood her ground, squeezing her eyes shut as she spoke. "I-I'm here to fight you."

Cackles erupted from the crowd, their taunting laughter ringing in Hope's ear. Behind her, there was a groan. It was Darius. And behind him, the security guard attempted to enter the ring. Victor shook his head and held his hand out.

"Leave her." He smiled wide. "If she wants to box, she can. I don't discriminate. And I never run from a fight." He motioned to the referee, whose sweat patches had now covered the entirety of his shirt.

"But this, this isn't in the rules..." The referee nervously pulled at his bowtie.

"So tonight, we'll write new rules."

"B-but the girl needs gloves."

"Do you have gloves?" Victor glanced at Hope's bare fists.

Hope shook her head.

"Well," he slid the gloves from his hand and handed them to his handlers. "We'll have to do this bare-fisted."

"Well, what do you know, folks?" The announcer entered the ring again. "You're getting a bonus show! Fighting the Fear today, sans gloves, we have....erm. What's your name? Weight? Record?"

"It's Hope Obiako, one-hundred and twenty-five pounds, undefeated because this is my first fight."

"Fighting out of the red corner, weighing in at one-hundred and twenty-five pounds and currently undefeated, Hooooope Obiaaaakooooo, ladies and gentlemen." The crowd jeered and howled in response as Hope bumped fists with the Fear and took to her corner, where Darius sat hunched on his stool.

"Hope, please, this is crazy—" Darius grabbed her wrist.

"I have to do this." Hope shook him away.

The bell rang, indicating the start of the fight. Hope and the Fear lunged towards each other, with Hope staying just out of his long arm's reach. *Stay out of the danger zone*, she thought. The Fear stepped forward, and Hope stepped back, allowing his jabs to breeze past—dangerously close to her face. *Never stop moving*. She bobbed and danced around him, her small body narrowly missing his punches. *Attack the body.* She ducked and punched him in the chest. He stopped to look down in disbelief.

"This is unbelievable, folks. Hope Obiako has landed the first punch of the fight, hitting the Fear square in the chest." The announcer's voice was nearly drowned out by the cheers in the crowd.

The amused smirk left the Fear's face and was replaced by a determined scowl. He charged at Hope, reeling his arm back to hit her at full force. She quickly ducked, allowing the force of his punch to send him flying forward.

Time slowed in that moment. As the Fear's body stumbled over hers, Hope looked up, and their eyes met. A look of horror washed over his face. He knew he was vulnerable. Hope wound her arm back, then her fist sliced through the air, hitting the Fear in the jaw with a crack. His body fell backward with a thump onto the ring floor. The crowd went silent. The referee emerged again, counting to ten with his fingers. The Fear didn't move. Only his chest slowly rose and fell.

As Hope was announced the winner, she could see the mouths of the audience gaping open, and their bodies jumped and thrashed like chimps. She knew they were cheering, howling even, but she couldn't hear it. As her arm was lifted up and a championship belt placed on her shoulder, she couldn't feel it. And as Darius slunk away, embarrassed, she didn't stop him. She was overtaken with something she hadn't felt in years. Something she thought she'd never feel again. She was actually proud of herself. She had accomplished something. Something real.

CHAPTER 10

— · —

THE THERAPIST

Early the next morning, Hope awoke with a start. A sharp pain shot through her right arm, culminating at her knuckles. She eased out of her couch-bed, wiping the sleep from her eyes with her left hand. She had punched Fear in the face. Right in the kisser. And she was victorious, but all she could think about was poor Darius, slinking away into the shadows defeated.

There was a knock at the door.

"Coming."

Hope crept to the front door, cradling her knuckles and wincing in pain with each step. She opened the door, revealing a buzzing swarm of reporters holding microphones and flashing cameras, snapping her every move.

"Hope Obiako, can we get a statement for Sports Illuminated?"

"Well, I'm not sure what to say, I've never read your magazine—"

"How long did you train before your Earth-shattering match against the Fear?"

"About three days. How'd you find my address—"

"Did you coordinate this stunt with Darius Smith?"

Hope shook her head. "Stunt? No, no, Darius didn't have anything to do with—"

"Did you know the Fear had suffered a concussion during his previous fight with the Kid Wonder?"

"What?"

The reporter nearest her thrust something into Hope's hands. It was a newspaper titled "The Daily Day", and right on the front cover was a glamor shot of Hope, next to a photo of Victor Sanchez. The headline read, "The Fear Suffers Concussion And Passes Out At Open Fight Night!", with a byline that read: "Is This Young Lady's Punch to Blame? Probably Not. But It Sure Didn't Help."

Normally, Hope would have felt a number of emotions. Firstly, horror at having punched an already concussed man. Secondly, embarrassed for not actually winning, but instead, all she could muster up was confusion and a single thought—*Have I ever taken a glamor shot before?*

She hadn't. Hope hated taking photos so much that, over time, she'd learned many stealthy ways to shield her face from the camera's intrusive lens. Whether it be well-placed hat brims, unfortunate bangs, or a smartly timed sneeze, she hadn't taken a proper photo since she was five. Something didn't feel right, and an oddness lingered in the air. Then she thought of Darius again.

"I'm sorry, I have to go." Hope shut the door, leaving the reporters outside, throwing their hands up in frustration.

Hope picked up her phone and dialed Darius' number, listed on his card. She'd almost forgotten about it, had it not been conveniently sticking out of her shirt's breast pocket. Not the shirt on her body, but a shirt that she had strewn on the floor days before.

The phone rang once before Darius answered.

"Darius Smith speaking."

"Hey, it's Hope."

Hope's greeting was followed by an uncomfortably long silence before he answered again. "Hello, Hope."

"I'm calling because, well, I'm-I'm sorry. I didn't mean to steal your thunder." Hope noticed a bright flash from her window. She turned and spotted a reporter shooting stealthy photos. She frowned and snapped the window shade closed.

"Oh, but you did. You came ready to fight. I could see it in your eyes. You meant it."

"I suppose I did mean to fight. But, I thought you'd win—I mean, I was hoping. Then I wanted to have my turn after."

"It's fine."

"Turns out, the Fear actually passed out from a concussion, and there's no way I—"

"Enjoy your win."

"But...I didn't *really* win. That's why I called."

Another silence. "Listen, I don't need another beatdown on top of the one I already got. I've got other things to deal with."

"What? Darius, no—"

"I've got to get ready for work. Be easy." The phone clicked, and the line went dead. He'd hung up on her.

With an ego almost as bruised as her swollen fist, Hope decided she was in the mood for tea. She boiled water and steeped a tea bag into her last clean cup. She spooned honey into her drink, as smooth and sweet as Darius' voice, and stirred.

As Hope sipped, her thoughts raced, and she couldn't get Darius' final words out of her head. *Be easy.* She knew that was Darius-speak for "I never want to see you on my bus again", and she was devastated by the thought. Not even tea could wash away the feeling of guilt that sat uncomfortably in the pit of Hope's stomach. She wanted so badly to tell someone, anyone, about her feelings. About the book. About the Fear. About Darius.

Hope spotted the catalyst for her current misery, *How to Be a Better Adult*, lying face down by her feet. *Stupid book*, she thought, before kicking it under her couch-bed with her heel.

Soon, her guilt morphed into a dull, familiar pang of loneliness. She thought to call Amber but shook the idea away as soon as it came. Amber witnessed death every day at her job, and even still, she surely dealt with the same workplace troubles that had plagued Hope. She didn't want to burden her with any more worries.

Hope laid back on her couch-bed, investigating the plastered bumps on her low ceiling. Calling her family was out of the question, of course. For all they knew, Hope was a big shot, saving up money to fund their lives when they grew too old and weary to work. Had they known she was newly unemployed and punching grown men in the face, they'd buy her a one-way flight back to Nigeria—a country she'd been twenty-five years removed from. Not that she minded that outcome. It was the look of disappointment in her parents' eyes that she was staving off.

Hope's loneliness sat on her chest, counting the ceiling bumps right along with her until it became too heavy to bear. She sighed and slipped on her sneakers, readying herself for the onslaught of reporters outside. But when she opened the door to leave, they were all gone.

♡♡♡

"Hope?" Dr. Marley sat on his stool, looking up at a sullen Hope standing in his office doorway. "Did we have an appointment today?"

Dr. Marley's therapy practice was located in a rundown commercial office building, half an hour away from Hope's condo. There were no receptionists or waiting rooms, just dozens of doors, each housing a different small business. Dr. Marley's door was nestled between a failing tech startup run by two brothers and a possibly unlicensed acupuncturist. Hope often wondered if Dr. Marley himself was an actual doctor, or if he was even licensed at all, but decided it didn't matter in the grand scheme of things.

"No, but I was hoping to see you if you have the time."

Dr. Marley shuffled through a few papers on his desk and checked the time on his watch.

"You've got me for about thirty minutes." He motioned towards his worn gray couch. "Please, have a seat."

Hope sat, sinking into the couch. It was steeped in a strong, stale, musky scent. Like a thrift store covered in cheap men's cologne.

Dr. Marley grabbed his clipboard and flipped through a few pages until he landed on what Hope assumed was her documentation.

"Last we chatted, you were excited about a big meeting." He looked up at Hope with his droopy eyes. "So, how did it go?"

Hope took a deep breath. "Dr. Marley, I'm seeing things, ominous messages. And I found this strange book on my doorstep and then...then I won a boxing match. But not really and..." Hope shifted in her seat. "...and I think I've lost a friend but...I'm afraid I've lost my wits as well."

Dr. Marley sighed, and all the features of his face sagged downward. Gravity took a special interest in his drooping eye bags. "Hope, are you projecting your negative worldview onto a mildly uncomfortable situation again?"

Hope looked down at her bandaged fist, a memento of her betrayal of Darius. "No, I don't think so."

"Well then, tell me where you think you've lost your wits. Have you checked under the bed?" Dr. Marley let out a howl of a laugh before devolving into a nervous cough after catching Hope's stoic face. "Just a bit of disarming humor."

Hope blinked away the tears that formed in her eyes and cracked a weak, lopsided smile to alleviate the tension in the room. "I've already checked there. Couldn't find them."

Dr. Marley's eyebags lifted in relief as he returned Hope's smile. "Honestly, Hope, tell me why you've come in today."

One year prior, Hope walked into Dr. Marley's office for the very first time. She'd never seen a therapist and didn't know what to expect, but she assumed he was in the business of listening. And after years of suppressing herself, Hope had a lot to say.

With his wild curls and big, wondrous eyes, Hope felt safe sharing what she perceived to be her strangest thoughts and feelings with the doctor. She spent the better half of an hour recounting how she felt outside of herself, how life was like a dream.

"...and I have no control over anything I do. I see myself moving. I *think* I'm making decisions. But really, I feel like I'm being pulled along on a string by something. Or, or someone." She let out a sigh of relief. She'd gotten every uncomfortable thought off her chest.

She looked up at the doctor, expectedly, but was met with a look of pity.

"Hope, life isn't a dream. *You're* in control of your actions. No one else."

It was at that moment that Hope learned some thoughts just weren't safe with anyone. Not even your therapist. She remembered this and settled on a more appropriate response to Dr. Marley's question.

"Honestly, I came in today because I was fired."

"I'm so sorry to hear that." Dr. Marley leaned forward, his face sagging with sympathy. "How does that make you feel?"

After a brief pause, Hope decided the truth was ok to share.

"I'm kind of angry."

Dr. Marley's red-tinted eyes gleamed with a look of pleasant surprise. He flipped through his clipboard and scratched down several notes. "Anger is a fine emotion, Hope. A very fine emotion."

"Is it?"

"Yes, of course. Anger drives people to action—that's something you struggle with, you know. Taking action." Dr. Marley spoke without taking his eyes off his notes. "And anger's also an emotion you've never mentioned in our sessions." Dr. Marley raised his head. His red eyes now focused on Hope. "What action is your anger driving you to take?"

"It's driving me to take charge of my life and punch fear in the face, so I can prove everyone wrong. So I can prove myself wrong." Hope looked down at her feet. She thought she shouldn't have used the word "punch".

"*Punch*, fear, *in* the...face." Dr. Marley spoke under his breath as he scribbled the statement in his notes. "Do you have a plan for how you'll change your self-image, Hope?"

"Your mantras have been very helpful, so I'll start there." This wasn't true, but Hope decided to offer the doctor a few crumbs of satisfaction.

A wide smile spread across Dr. Marley's face. Hope continued.

"And I suppose I'll have to take things a step at a time." She paused to think for a moment. "I need to find a new job. A better job."

"That's an excellent first step, Hope. You can rebuild your confidence and regain control of your life."

"Thank you, Dr. Marley. You're always so helpful," she lied.

Dr. Marley's sleepy face lit up. "Always a pleasure. Please keep me informed on your progress."

"Of course!" Hope smiled.

"Alright." Dr. Marley clasped his hands together. "That'll be one-hundred-and-fifty dollars. Cash or card today?"

CHAPTER 11

THE RECRUITER

In the week that passed, Hope stumbled upon *Mesmerize Your Life,* a book detailing how to will the universe to do your bidding simply by writing down your wants and dreams. It was a concept similar to Dr. Marley's mantras, but not quite. *This* method of manifestation relied on creating a better future. Not lying to yourself about the conditions of the present.

The author of the book was once destitute, down-in-the-dumps, and broke but had willed a life of wealth, fulfillment, and adventure through journaling and envisioning himself in the place he wanted his future self to be. Soon, time and opportunity met, and his dream of becoming a world-renowned hypnotist came true.

With this in mind, Hope sat cross-legged on her curiously scented carpet with a pen in hand, writing down her current wish in a half-used journal she found on her bookshelf.

I want an amazing, life-changing career.

Hope felt very silly writing such a request, but she thought it was easier to ask for than immense riches or something as unattainable as inner peace. Plus, Hope considered manifestation to be a safer method of self-improvement, as opposed to a book that encouraged her to pummel professional athletes.

I want an amazing, life-changing career.

She wrote it again for good measure, then snapped her journal shut, ignoring the text on the bottom of the page that hadn't been there before; *You're wasting your pen's ink, Hope. No one will hire you in the state you're in now. Open the book.* While the words were a bit foreboding, she couldn't waste any more time focusing on things that weren't really there. She had an important appointment that she couldn't miss.

"So, Hope, it looks like you only have one job on your resume? And...a single boxing match win? Do you have any more work history you may be forgetting? Maybe internships during college?" The job recruiter, Elaine, evaded eye contact and clicked the point of her pen in and out as she spoke. Hope imagined it was a nervous tick. Elaine wasn't very good at pretending.

While the rest of her colleagues sat up straight, exuding confidence in sleek, professional outfits, Elaine sat slightly hunched. She'd missed a button on her shirt, right in front of her bosom, throwing off the symmetry of her blouse. A single strand of red hair wisped across her forehead.

"I never interned, but I did work as a receptionist at a motel for a little while. And a sales associate at Lowell Potter."

"The shoe outlet?"

Hope nodded.

"I see. What about volunteering?"

"No, no volunteering. I just worked odd jobs through school…" Hope peered at the resume in Elaine's hands. "But did you see I was an Account Specialist for William Hensley and Associates for—"

"For one year. Yes, I see that. And it's slightly impressive." Elaine's pen-clicking abruptly stopped. "But I'm afraid it's not enough to prove your skill and competency. How did you manage to land this position with no prior work experience?"

The truth was Hope had peppered her old resume with lies, then warned Amber and her mother that they'd be receiving calls to confirm her work history. Amber was listed as the hiring manager at a marketing firm in the midwest, while Hope's mother was the CEO of a relatively unknown publishing company. Both played their roles flawlessly. Hope would have kept up the charade this time around as well, but after reading about how increased competition in the job market had led to more scrupulous background-checking processes, she thought she ought to be truthful.

"I suppose they liked me." Hope chuckled a bit.

"Well, in this economy, being liked is not enough." Stone-faced, Elaine slid Hope's resume back to her. "I'd suggest doing less boxing and more volunteering or contract work to beef up your resume. With how it looks now, you'll be hard-pressed to find employment of a similar caliber."

Normally Hope would have answered with a cheerful, "Ok, thank you!" and she did, but the tone of Elaine's voice, the slight condescension, rubbed Hope the wrong way. She added, "You missed a button," and watched with satisfaction as Elaine's face burned red with embarrassment.

♡♡♡

Downstairs, Hope sat in the lobby, watching for the bus through its tall glass walls, with likability on her mind. *Is the currency of being well-regarded really worthless?* she thought. Her faded orange book had gotten her as far as it did in her career, but even still, she was so easily cast aside and discarded by Liz and Monica. *Or maybe being likable isn't enough when—*

"Hope?" A familiar voice called out, interrupting her thoughts.

Hope looked up to see Alex poking his head inside the glass double doors of the lobby. He wore a more relaxed outfit than she was used to. Khaki slacks and a baby blue button-up. His smile was more relaxed, even. Behind him stood two similarly dressed men smiling and chatting and checking their expensive watches.

"Funny seeing you here. I was just reading a write-up about you in *Sports Illuminated*. Really inspiring stuff. I didn't know you boxed in your spare time."

Hope's heart fluttered from embarrassment. She thought to ask for more details about the article but couldn't bare feeling any more awkward than she already did.

Alex waved at the men waiting behind him, signaling for them to continue on without him.

"I was just on my way back to the office. Took some of the seventh-floor guys to Cafe Dumont for lunch. Decided to walk since we get hour-long lunch breaks now." Alex stepped into the lobby and took in its surroundings. "What're you doing here? Promotion not panning out the way you expected?"

"Promotion?" Hope failed to hide her confusion.

"You *weren't* promoted?"

"You *were?*"

"Yeah, I've got an office on the sixth floor now. Dale's a real stand-up guy. And they open the windows!" Alex sat next to Hope. "But what happened? Are your boxing dreams taking you down a different career path?"

For a moment, an uncomfortable feeling rose up to Hope's chest. She fought to keep it anchored down.

"I...was fired." She was careful to control the shakiness of her voice.

"*Fired!?*" A genuine look of bewilderment washed over Alex's face. His voice dropped to a whisper. "But why? We completed the Milton project."

"Maybe I just wasn't a culture fit." Hope decided to spare Alex from the guilt of knowing his lunch plans contributed to her demise.

"That makes no sense, why wouldn't you be?"

Monica's statement that "people" like Hope were expendable echoed through her skull as she pasted a warm smile on her face.

"I don't know. Not too many Account Specialists donning boxing gloves on the weekends, I guess."

Alex laughed. "Listen, I wanna keep seeing you win. There's an invite-only networking event tonight at Houlihan's, and I'd love to see you there. Places like this," he made a sweeping motion around the lobby, "won't lead you to greatness. Climbing the ladder is all about scratching expensive, well-connected backs and banking on them scratching yours in return."

"Well..." Hope hated networking events. She also squirmed at the thought of spending more time alone with Alex. Not because she disliked him. He made sure she couldn't. But because she was intimidated by him.

"Come on. I owe you a good time, at the very least. It'll be fun!"

Hope considered turning him down and sparing herself an evening of awkward silences and desperate scrambles to fill the gaps in conversation. Then she remembered she was unemployed, so she resigned.

"Ok, sure."

"Great." He smiled. "Just tell the man at the door that you're with me."

"Thanks, Alex."

"No problem. See you tonight!" Alex walked backwards towards the glass doors, smiling and waving goodbye. Hope smiled and waved as well. In the background, she watched her bus sputter away. It would be another hour before the next one arrived.

CHAPTER 12

— · —

THE NETWORKING EVENT

In the evening, Hope slipped into a pencil skirt, pointed heels, and a silky blouse that buttoned up to her neck. She felt a bit overdressed for an Irish pub but wanted to make a good first impression on any important people who may be in the room. She also slid pepper spray into her tiny purse, just in case.

By eight o'clock, Hope had transformed into a corporate professional once again. By eight-thirty, she was nervously waiting at the bus stop, bracing herself to see Darius for the first time since the fight.

When the bus slowed and the doors peeled open, there was a sleepy-looking woman sitting where Darius should have been. She looked down at Hope with her downturned eyes.

Hope couldn't catch her surprise in time, and an unenthused "Oh." slipped through her lips. "I thought Darius drove this route."

"Darius has taken some time off." The woman answered, purposely withholding any more information and almost daring Hope to pry so she could shut her down.

"I see." Hope dropped change into the box and sat in the front row. She glanced at the woman in the rearview mirror, hoping to catch a friendly glance back, but she kept her tired eyes on the road.

With a name like Houlihan's, Hope expected your usual Irish pub. The ones with gaudy shiny paper shamrocks plastered on the wall, bar food that was overwhelmingly mediocre, and cheap drink specials for every day of the week. Instead, to her surprise, she was greeted at the door by a tall man in a fancy suit jacket with gold embellishments.

When Hope mentioned Alex's name, the man smiled widely, opened one of two wrought iron front doors, and called her "madam". It was all so very upscale, and suddenly Hope felt extremely out of place. An establishment like this didn't call for a pencil skirt and a button-up. A place like Houlihan's deserved a little black dress with a plunging neckline. Hope unbuttoned her blouse as far as she could while still maintaining an air of coyness.

Houlihan's was even more impressive on the inside. In the center of the room was a giant, golden bar that wrapped around a shimmering diamond-like column. Square, red leather booths lined the walls, and small, golden, reflective round tables were peppered throughout while gentle string music filled the air. This wasn't just a bar. It was a royal palace, and Hope was a poor pauper infiltrating the bourgeoisie upper class. As she was taking it all in, she spotted Alex walking toward her.

"Hope! You made it! Come grab a drink with me!" Alex shouted from a slight distance. Hope's ears warmed with embarrassment as pairs of eyes turned one by one to look in her direction.

Behind the bar, a tall, slender man with suspenders and a handlebar mustache did a double-take as the pair approached.

"Ah, Alex!" He put down the glass he was polishing and reached out to give Alex a handshake. "Haven't seen you in a while. How have you been?"

"Niall!" Alex shook his hand. "I've been alright, swamped at work these days. Just got a promotion, so you know how that goes. Gotta prove myself all over again."

"A promotion? Look at you moving on up! Not that I expected any less." Niall smiled widely, then glanced at a visibly tense Hope. "And who is this pretty young thing?" He winked at her.

Alex laughed. "This is Hope." He looked at Hope now. "Hope, this is Niall, a good friend of mine."

"Nice to meet you." Hope smiled and held her hand out for a shake. Instead, Niall took it and kissed it. She instinctively snatched it away.

Niall laughed heartily. "I see someone's a bit uptight! I know the perfect cure for that." He winked at Alex before pouring several bottles of alcoholic beverages with names like "Passion", "Captain Trudeau", and "Eclipse" into two glasses of orange juice. Hope was uncomfortable now, and she patted her bag, hoping to feel the outline of her pepper spray.

"Here you go!" He slid the drinks in front of the two. Alex pulled out his wallet to pay, but Niall held up his hand to refuse. "It's on the house! Tell your friend, Stacey, I said hello and that she still owes me that date."

"You know Stacey, she loves to play hard to get. But I'll put in a good word for you."

"That's my boy." Niall looked at Hope while pointing to Alex. "This one's always looking out for his friends. Don't know a better guy."

"As long as you keep adding me to the guestlist for these events, I'll introduce you to every woman I know!" The two laughed.

After saying his goodbyes, Alex picked up both glasses, and Hope followed him to a small golden table.

"You don't have to drink this if you don't want to." He must have sensed her uncomfortableness. She didn't like that.

"Of course I want to!" Hope grabbed the glass and downed its contents. She quickly realized that was a mistake. The taste stung her tongue and burned her throat as it made its way down to her gut. It burned there too, but not in a comforting way. Her insides were on fire. *Why on Earth did people drink hard liquor?* She recoiled a bit from the shock of it all and looked up to find Alex staring at her, his eyes full of amusement.

"You don't drink often, do you?" He said with a knowing smile.

"No, actually, it's been years," Hope admitted. "And this tastes like gasoline."

Alex laughed and pulled a bar straw from a small black box at the center of the table. He plunked it into Hope's drink. "Maybe that'll make it go down easier."

Hope smiled and took a sip. It was still disgusting, but she gave Alex a thumbs-up of approval anyway.

"So, when does this networking event start?" she asked.

"You're looking at it. The Association of Exceptional Marketing Professionals rents this place out once a month for their Rising Stars mixer. I'm not part of the Association yet, but a few more bouts of elbow-rubbing, and I'm sure I'll get the formal invite."

Hope looked around at the people in the bar. Both the men and women wore sharp suits and sleek hairstyles and stuck closely to their small groups, with the exception of a few lone attendees who circled around, watching the clusters of people with hawkish eyes.

"People are just warming up now," Alex explained. "Once they get a nice buzz going, they'll start to mingle."

Hope nodded her head and took another sip of her drink. If she was going to be chatting with total strangers, she also needed a nice buzz.

"So, before we start chatting up total strangers, tell me about yourself, Hope. I feel like we never got to know each other on that stuffy third floor. Other than boxing, what do you do for fun?"

The questions "tell me about yourself" and "what do you do for fun" were ones Hope encountered many times in a number of her books. They were basic networking questions. Amateur, almost. Hope was surprised Alex didn't jumpstart the conversation with something more advanced.

"Well, I read."

"Oh?" Alex looked awfully impressed, which bothered Hope for reasons she couldn't quite articulate. "What do you read?"

"A bit of everything. But mostly business profiles, self-help...and fantasy." Hope sighed. "Sometimes, I wish I could just make a home for myself in one of my books." Hope was feeling light-headed and warm now, and words were spilling out of her mouth faster than she could screen them. She was buzzed. "I'm sorry. Was that strange?"

"Not at all." Alex smiled. "And if it is, then there's plenty of strange things I'd wish for myself..." He took a sip of his drink.

"Like what? You've got a nice car, a nice promotion, and a nice face already." As soon as the words left Hope's lips, her buzz left with it, leaving her feeling completely sober and embarrassed.

Alex laughed. "Well, thank you. You've got a nice face yourself." He winked. "You'll have to recommend some books to me one of these days."

Hope blushed. She wasn't sure if he was flirting. She wasn't sure if *she* was flirting. But they continued to drink, and, as much as Hope hated the taste, she enjoyed the feeling of being somewhat carefree.

♡♡♡

After a few drinks together, Alex wished Hope luck and went off to "work the room", leaving her alone at their golden table. It wasn't long before she was approached. Networking was like speed dating, and as quick as they'd come, they'd go, but not without leaving behind a business card for Hope's collection. At this rate, her tiny purse would be bursting at the seams by the end of the night.

A balding older man left her with a parting gift of not one but two cards. One with his business information and the other with his personal number, which gave Hope the creeps. Once he turned to hone in on his next target, Hope closed her eyes and let out a heavy sigh. Her drinks were wearing off, and she was growing tired from keeping up appearances.

Thunk!

Hope looked up to see two drinks sitting in front of her. Across from her, holding the glasses, stood a tall, stunning woman in a slinky black dress. Her thick braids cascaded down her back, and the gold flecks of light from the decor reflected on her smooth skin. She hovered over Hope with a mischievous smile on her face.

"Something tells me you need this." Her thick southern drawl reminded Hope of Darius. "Mind if I sit, sweetheart?"

"Not at all."

The woman sat. She was even more beautiful up close. Hope couldn't keep her eyes off her.

"Name's Mona. How about yourself?"

"Hope. Nice to meet you." Hope's voice trembled a bit from nerves. She readied her arsenal of networking questions. "How'd you hear about this event—"

Mona waved the question away. "We don't have to go through that whole song and dance. I'm tired of the bullshit, aren't you?"

Hope nodded. She wasn't just tired, she was exhausted. And all it took was a single question to unzip the suffocating social constraints she'd been wearing for far too long. She exhaled, finally feeling a bit of comfort.

Mona leaned back in her seat and looked around, taking in her surroundings. "Looks like we're the only two sisters in this whole place."

"I'm used to being the *only* one," Hope sighed. "This would be considered a multicultural event at my last job."

Mona laughed, but not in the way you laugh at things that are funny. "Isn't that a shame? There was a time I thought I could *never* get used to this. Now I'm putting on an Oscar-worthy performance Monday through Friday." Mona took a deep swig of her drink. "I'm supposed to be on vacation, and they're still sending me to these damn networking events."

"I understand. By the end of the day, I almost forget who I am. I don't think I even know anymore..."

Mona raised her eyebrows ever so slightly, which made Hope feel uneasy. She stopped herself and took a drink instead. She'd been on the brink of sharing too much. Mona leaned back in her chair. "You wanna know something?"

Hope nodded.

"I studied at the most prestigious school in this country. I work my ass off every day." Mona leaned forward to emphasize her words. "I'm not one to brag. I just want you to understand that I'm *very* good at my job. But every day, I'm tested. If I didn't come here today, they were gonna find a way to terminate me."

"But *why?*" Hope asked although she knew why. She fought back the memory of her own firing. She'd been doing well suppressing her anger and didn't want to regress.

"Oh, you know why." Mona shifted in her chair. "I still managed to climb the ranks, though, and I'm in line for a senior position now—as I deserve."

"So how'd you do it?" Hope was hanging off of Mona's every word now.

"I'm blackmailing my boss."

Hope nearly choked on her drink. "Really?!"

"Of course. One thing I've learned about corporate? *Everyone* plays dirty. And with a smile on their face, too. You see that man right there?" She motioned towards a short, bald man laughing at a table full of other balding men. "He's backstabbing his best friend and planning on stealing his company. And he'll succeed, too. But he'll run it into the ground after a year."

Mona continued, "And that lady right there? The one with the short hair?" She motioned to a blonde woman with a pixie cut, chatting up a table full of young men in ill-fitting suits, "She's charming her way into learning trade secrets, then she'll sell 'em to larger companies so they can crush startups. She's gonna make bank, but it'll catch up to her."

Hope shook her head in disbelief. She looked around at the corporate vultures circling them, firmly shaking hands and flashing toothy grins as they sized up their targets.

"I don't think I'll ever be able to navigate this world."

"You could," Mona eyed Hope in a way that made her slightly uncomfortable. "Or, maybe you couldn't."

Before Hope could process the meaning behind her words, Mona stood to her feet.

"But it was nice networking with you, Hope. Maybe I'll see you at another one of these." She handed Hope a card for her collection, then strutted away into a sea of sharks.

Hope looked down at the black card in her hand. It read "Mona Kitt - Futurist" and, in much tinier letters below, "Kline Turner Solutions".

Kline Turner Solutions. Hope had heard that name before. No, she'd read it. In the Milton Report. She mentally trudged through the deepest pits of her memory banks to retrieve a single sentence. A fragment of a sentence, actually: "Kline Turner Solutions, risk mitigation services; Eighty billable hours".

"So, Hope, what do you do?" A red-haired man with a splattering of freckles across his face approached Hope after

Mona departed. The man informed Hope of his name, but she'd forgotten because, at that point, she was quite intoxicated.

"I'm a...a former Account Specialist at William Hensley and Associates."

"Oh, woooow," The corners of his mouth dropped, and his brows lifted into a look of interest and impress. "*The* William Hensley and Associates?"

"Yup," she answered. "The one, the one and only." Hope felt her body sway a bit, and she held onto her table for balance. "What do you do?"

As soon as he began rambling off about accounting something or other, Hope instantly regretted asking. She zoned out and discreetly let her eyes scan the room behind him. She noticed Alex in a far corner, chatting with Mona. Every few seconds, they'd laugh together, flashing their perfect white teeth in unison. Together they resembled movie stars.

Hope snapped back to reality right as the redhead man wrapped up his spiel, professing his love for crunching numbers.

"So, where'd you go to school?" He asked.

"Westbrook University." She answered, only half paying attention. She watched over his shoulder as Alex and Mona made their way to the bar.

"No way!" The man exclaimed. "I was a falcon too!" He crossed his hands until they formed a bird shape and wiggled his fingers.

Hope smiled and returned the gesture, attempting to match his excitement out of politeness.

"Small world." He continued, "Not often you find two mid-westerners in the big city." He winked. Hope winced.

She ran into mid-westerners all the time. And he probably did too. That's small talk for you. *It's all bullshit.*

"Right? Totally small!" she echoed.

"Wait, I think I knew of a Hope. What's your last name? What year'd you graduate? Maybe we had a class together!" he asked.

"It's Obiako," *Shoot, why did I tell him my real name?* She hoped he wouldn't recognize her. Hope quickly continued, "I graduated three years ago. You?" She had to keep remembering to return his questions back to him, although she was far from interested and uncomfortably drunk.

"Oh wow! I graduated last year and—wait...did you say "Obiako"? Are you related to Dr. Peter Obiako?"

Darn it. He knew her father. There were two types of Westbrook students—ones who had taken her father's class and others who hadn't. The former who usually had a very strong opinion about him and his teaching methods.

"You don't need Facebook! You only need to face your books!" He'd shout in a strong Nigerian accent that would leave weak-minded students cowering, herself included.

"Oh no," she lied. "I get that a lot, though. It's a...common Nigerian name."

"Oh, I see. Well, you're better off not being related to that guy. He was crazy! Always screaming at us in that accent..." He laughed.

As she heard this random man insult her father, a feeling of shame washed over her. She couldn't believe she'd denied knowing him, as harsh as he could be.

"Well, I heard he's a great professor. He's passionate."

"I wouldn't call that passion. I'd call it insanity." He laughed again.

Suddenly the rage Hope had been suppressing for weeks bubbled inside of her, right alongside the many mixed drinks and wine. Her mind went hazy, and the drunkenness possessed her. Without thinking, she cocked her fist back and punched the redhead man in the face.

CHAPTER 13

— • —

DIG YOUR WAY OUT OF DEBT

The next morning, Hope awoke with a throbbing headache and a box of Chinese take-out on her lap. The room spun as she took in her surroundings. The pile of dishes, the peeling paint, the musty smell. She was in her condo. She was also fully dressed. That was a relief, as she had no recollection of how she'd gotten home, but she couldn't forget that punch. She replayed the scene in her mind like a cursed loop. The redheaded man holding his face and threatening to sue. The balding old man with his mouth agape. And Alex keeping his distance, watching like a spectator from afar.

Waves of anxiety rippled through Hope's chest as she sat up and searched for her cell phone. She anticipated a message from Alex, scolding her and saying he never wanted to see her again. Instead, there was a single missed text from her landlord, Lisa.

Lisa Bellows: I haven't received your rent check.

Hope's heart pounded in her chest. She knew it was coming eventually, but the message stressed her out nonetheless. She responded.

Hope Obiako: Sorry Lisa I've been swamped with work! I thought it got to you already, I sent the check out last Friday.

Hope hadn't sent the rent check last Friday. She didn't have enough money to pay it, and wouldn't until she found a new job.

Lisa Bellows: No. Haven't received it.

Hope Obiako: Maybe it got lost in the mail again. I'm out of town on a business trip for W&H, I can just bring the check over to you when I return.

Sometimes Hope felt terrible lying, but she reminded herself that she lived in less-than-stellar conditions and never complained. The least Lisa could do was let her pay rent a few weeks late. Right?

Lisa Bellow: Ok.

Hope fell back onto her couch-bed and let out a quiet sigh of relief. Another month with a roof over her head, but with no money and no job prospects, she had no way to pay rent. A lump sat in Hope's throat, which could've very well been remnants of the sesame chicken she'd apparently eaten.

I can't fall any further, she thought. *At this rate, I'll be working as a sign twirler for a used car dealership.*

Don't be like that. Sign-twirling is a respectable and physically taxing career that you're, quite frankly, unqualified for. A voice called out from nowhere.

"Who's there?" Hope sat back up, afraid that someone might have snuck in as she was laid out intoxicated.

No one. Just the voice in your head. Well, the other one. It's a little crowded in here."

"It's happened. I've really lost my mind."

No, you haven't lost it. It's right here with me. The Voice explained. *Now listen up. I haven't much time before the alcohol completely leaves your system.*

Hope fell back onto her couch-bed, throwing her sense of reality at absurdity's feet.

"Sure. What's up?" She remembered why she wasn't fond of drinking.

You were given a gift, and you've just thrown it away like a piece of garbage. That's very ungrateful of you.

"If you're talking about that book, it was ruining my life—"

You're ruining your life. Who told you to drink so much? You made that choice and now look at you. That book is the manual you've always wanted, isn't it? You've got answers right there, under your squalid couch.

"Couch-*bed*." Hope corrected the voice.

Sorry, under your squalid couch-bed.

"Voice?"

Yes?

"Are you the one who's been writing those ominous messages? Not that I mind too much, well, that's a lie, they're really throwing off my confidence. Could you ease back a bit?"

I guess I've been quite ominous, haven't I?

Hope nodded before realizing the Voice couldn't see her. "Ah, yes, kind of," she answered.

Ok, sure. I can scale it back, but I'm only trying to help... The voice gently faded until it was gone.

Being the obedient and still slightly tipsy person she was, Hope dropped to her knees and fished *How to Be a Better Adult* from the dark and harrowing depths of under-her-couch-bed. *It is a bit squalid under here*, she thought while wiping away the bits of dust that had accumulated on its maroon cover. As she held the book in her hands, a bruised and beaten Darius staggered across her mind.

Hope quickly shook away her guilt, letting the image of Darius fade away along with her intoxication.

He'll come around eventually, she thought, because it was also a very adult thing to do, and he was even more seasoned in adulthood than she. He was well in his thirties, after all. And he'd had his chance. Whether Hope wanted to admit it or not, she'd felt victorious standing on that stage with her fists in the air. Fighting the Fear gave her a flash of confidence, and she desperately needed another win.

Maybe the Voice was right. No, the Voice *was* right. Why continue making shitty choices when she could give her life to the pages of How to Be a Better Adult? Laying her hesitation to the side, Hope opened the book to page three. The formerly blank page was now filled with text:

Dig Your Way Out of Debt

Are you currently burdened by the shackles of debt? Overwhelmed by your responsibilities? Fumbling through your taxes year after year?

Adulthood means taking on more financial responsibilities than ever before. Actually, no, you don't take them on. They're unceremoniously piled on top of you, bill by bill. One day your only concern is turning in your simple homework assignments, then you blink and you're paying for rent, a car note, and insurance?? None of it is fair.

No, you didn't get yourself into this hole. But there is a way out. It'll be messy, but in the game of life you can't be afraid to get your hands dirty. So, roll up your sleeves and dig your way out of debt.

Action Item: *Dig your way out of debt.*

The next page was blank. But Hope expected as much. This time she didn't question what the author's words could mean, and she didn't wait around for a sign. She knew, almost instinctually, what her next move should be.

"Hope! You off the phone? Can I flush the toilet? Or will it mess up your plans for the day?" A voice called out from the bathroom, interrupting Hope's thoughts.

"Voice? You're back?" Hope excitedly asked, hungry for more guidance.

The bathroom door swung open, revealing the silhouette of a tall woman in a baggy t-shirt standing in the doorframe. "Back? I never left."

"*Mona?*"

"So, can I flush? You told me about your unfortunate plumbing situation."

"Yeah, uh, go ahead."

"Cool." Mona stepped into the tiny bathroom, flushed, and washed her hands. Her long braids were tied up into a lopsided bun, and she wore Hope's oversized college t-shirt, a stark difference from her sleek little black dress—and even still, she resembled an off-duty model.

Hope watched in disbelief as Mona floated to the kitchen, reached into her mounting pile of dishes and, effortlessly washed a single glass, then filled it with water. She handed it to Hope and plopped onto the couch-bed behind her.

"Here you go, sweetheart. You know, you should really do your dishes."

Hope took the glass. "Um, thank you?"

"Figured you'd have a major hangover."

Hope paused for a moment. "I'm sorry but did we—"

"Sleep together? No, we didn't. Did you want to or something?"

"Oh, I-I was just—"

Mona smirked and continued. "I got you some food and drove you home. After you knocked Nick out, I knew you weren't making it on your own."

Hope looked down and shrank with embarrassment.

"Girl, don't worry, I work with him, and he's an asshole. I'm glad you punched him, although I never would've predicted that." Mona narrowed her eyes. "But now I know why I couldn't see it."

"What do you mean? Couldn't see what?"

"Your future." Mona reached over and plucked *How to Be a Better Adult* from Hope's hands.

Hope, in a panic, reached for the book. "How do you know about that?"

Mona lifted it out of reach. "Calm down, love. *You* showed me last night and—" She paused in thought. "Wait, you don't remember anything, do you?"

Hope shook her head no.

"I see." Mona stood to her feet and leaned on Hope's precious bookshelf, flipping through the pages of the book. "You told *me* you jumped in a boxing ring with no gloves on. And I told *you* I could see the future of everyone in that room."

Hope shook her head. "So...you're *psychic*?"

"Psychic?" Mona sucked her teeth and batted the suggestion away with her hand. "I'm a *futurist*. I study the facts, figures, and everyday happenings that create the future as it unfolds. And like I told you, I'm *very* good at my job."

"That's what you do for W&H..." Hope recalled the fragment of a sentence she'd read about Mona's employer.

"Yup, future consultation. We're on retainer." Mona turned to scan the colorful spines on Hope's bookshelf. "There's about ten of us in my department that can calculate every move a person will make. Most people? Easy to read. We can see at least a decade into their future."

Mona continued, pulling a pink book from the shelf and examining it. "And then there's the unhinged ones, like my boss. No one else in the department can read him but me, and even so, I can only predict about a month into his future. It was juuuust enough to know he'd cheat on his wife with his secretary. Typical rich, bored, White man shit."

"Can you predict your own future?" Hope was curious to learn more about Mona's abilities.

"...I can." Mona's expression darkened. "It used to change depending on what choices I made. But now, no matter what, it stays the same. It's...inevitable."

"So, what is it?" Hope leaned in, oblivious to the change in Mona's mood.

Mona cleared her throat. "Boring stuff..."

Hope remembered Mona chatting with Alex by the bar. Still hoping for a possible reconciliation, she asked, "What about Alex's future? Could you see it?"

"The guy with the teeth?" Mona rolled her eyes, "He's a loser, you deserve so much better." She turned to look at Hope. "But *your* future? I didn't see a thing. Just a gaping black hole. You know why that is?"

"I-I don't know...this is the first I've heard that I have no future." This was a lie. Hope's father had essentially told her the same when she broke the news of her changing career trajectory.

"You're dropping Pre-Pharmacy to study *English*?" Peter barked, slamming Hope's D-riddled report card down on the dining table between them.

Hope's tears held on for dear life, not daring to release and expose her weakness to her father. "I'm struggling in my science classes. I lost my scholarship. There's no way I'll get accepted into Pharmacy school. I just...I can't." Hope continued fighting her tears. "This is the better choice for me—"

"If you do this, you'll have no future."

"Peter, please!" Hope's mother, Tochi, called out from the kitchen, maintaining enough distance to allow Peter to exert his dominance but still close enough to offer Hope the support she needed. "Don't say something like that to our daughter."

"No, someone needs to tell her the truth! You have to focus and make choices for your future. Do this, and you'll ruin everything we've sacrificed for you."

Hope tuned out her father's berating, as she'd trained herself to do once he reached his overall point, but this time his words stuck with her. *She had no future.* As she walked across the graduation stage with her cap and gown, she saw only uncertainty at the other end. So she wasn't surprised in the slightest to hear she was future-less.

Mona held up her hand. "You're not future-less. Just because I can't see your future doesn't mean it isn't there, love."

"Maybe..." Hope's eyes widened as her mind suddenly birthed a thought that left her wrought with worry, "maybe you can't see my future because I'm gonna die soon."

"No. Death is bright. Warm. Absolute. This?" Mona held up *How to Be a Better Adult.* "Isn't that. It feels vague and chaotic and...unpredictable. *This* might be tampering with your future."

While Hope was happy to hear she wasn't dying, she was still a bit concerned. "What kind of chaos are we talking about?"

Mona, ignoring Hope's worrying, held up the pink book in her other hand. It was *The Taking of the Rose*, one of the worst books Hope had ever read. "How'd you like this book?" she asked, slightly laughing as she spoke.

"It was pretty good. Sagged a bit in the middle, but a solid effort from the writer." Hope recited a neutral review she'd read online.

"Why did you just do that?"

"Do what?"

"Lie. Why'd you just lie? Last night you told me this was the worst book you'd ever read."

Heat rushed to Hope's cheeks and ears. "I-I didn't want to be negative, I guess." She'd read in a book once that in social settings, positive people were always preferred over those who skewed more negatively.

Mona shook her head and slid the book back on the shelf. "These corporate folk have done a number on you, sis. Lie to them...not me." Mona leaned on the bookshelf and cracked open *How To Be a Better Adult*. Her eyes skimmed through the pages, taking in every printed word as an embarrassed Hope watched on. "Dig your way out of debt?"

"I know it seems ridiculous but—"

"You know what? If it's not my job, it's not my business. I've seen stranger things at Happy Hour with the Finance team." Mona snapped the book shut and handed it to Hope. "Do you have the time?"

Hope checked her cell phone. "It's eleven thirty—"

"Shit, I knew I'd be late to brunch, but not *this* late." Mona pulled her t-shirt over her head and slipped back into her slinky black dress from the evening before.

"Can you zip me up, love?"

"Sure thing."

As Hope zipped up Mona's dress, she reflected on her evening. She made it home, she was safe, and she seemed not to have done anything outrageously embarrassing, according to Mona. Yeah, maybe she didn't have a future, but at least networking was enough of a success, as she clearly made a new connection.

"Thanks, sweetheart." Mona sauntered to the front door before turning to face Hope again, "I don't mean to be forward, but...I'd like to see you again."

Hope smiled, happy to have made a new friend after losing Darius. "I'd love that."

"I'll be in touch." Mona returned her smile. "Good luck digging. And if you're looking for a shovel, you should try Kalston's."

CHAPTER 14

— ◦ —

THE GOLDEN SHOVEL

T hanks to Mona's suggestion, Hope found herself
scouring the shelves of her nearest home improvement
store—Kalston's. Kalston's was a large, bleak-looking warehouse
steeped in a dusty brown atmosphere. The heavy-duty metal
shelving was stocked with all sorts of gadgets and tools. Some
Hope recognized, but most she did not. And everyone in the store,
from the employees to the customers, lumbered about in steel-toe
boots while draped in variations of denim and flannel. Hope stood
out like a sore thumb in more ways than one.

Not wanting to look even more out of place, Hope pushed her
cart with purpose. Occasionally she'd stop to look at a power tool
or an appliance while rubbing her chin as if to say, '*I know exactly
what I want, but I'm mulling over my options.*'

"Ma'am? You need some help?" A burly, bearded man wearing a
bright orange vest approached. Tacked on his chest was a nametag
with "Bruce" scribbled on it.

"I'm just mulling over my options..." Hope quickly dropped her
facade, "but if you'd like to help, I was looking for a shovel to—"

"Wait a minute. Are you Hope, ugh..." he snapped his fingers to
activate his memory centers, "Obiako?"

"How'd you know my name?" Hope looked down to see if she also had a scribbled nametag tacked to her chest.

"How could I not? And even if I didn't, I'd know that fist." He motioned towards Hope's right hand. "Me and the boys saw you punch the Fear right in the face. We've even got your *Sports Illuminated* profile hanging up in the breakroom. We're big fans."

"Oh, right," Hope remembered Darius again. Moments like these should have been his.

"It was beautiful. Awe-inspiring. Y'know, right after I thought, if this little lady can stare down Fear just like that, what am I waiting for? After the fight, I skipped the pub and went straight home to apply to culinary school."

"That's amazing! I'm glad I could inspire you, but it's really Darius Smith who should be getting all the credit. He's the one who inspired me to—"

"Who?" Bruce shook his head and batted the question away as soon as he asked it. "Never mind that. You're a busy lady, and I won't be the guy to waste your time. If you need a shovel, I've got you. Follow me!"

Bruce turned to lead a somewhat guilt-ridden Hope through a maze of drill bits, window shades, and lawnmowers until they reached the lush, green Garden Center. The brown, industrial look of the rest of the store had no place here. Instead, rows of potted plants bursting with colorful flowers lined the walls and shelves, and tropical trees towered up toward the glass ceiling. Filtered sunlight bathed the center in a warm yellow glow.

"Now, we've got a shovel for all your gardening needs. We've got edging shovels, scoop shovels, handheld shovels, digging shovels—"

"That's what I need! A digging shovel."

Bruce stopped and looked back at Hope, his eyes beaming with excitement. "Oh, if it's a digging shovel you need, I've got the perfect one for ya."

He pulled out a stepping stool and reached up to the highest shelf, then extended even further to a shelf Hope couldn't see. When he descended from the ladder, he held a long, shiny, golden shovel in his hands. Its pointed tip gleamed in the Center's filtered sunlight. Hope admired the intricate etching that decorated its shaft and handle. The symbols looked otherworldly, like they'd been carved by beings from another time or space. Hope thought to inquire, but before she could ask what the carvings meant, Bruce spoke.

"This beauty is our Kalston brand luxury gold-plated digging shovel. We like to call her Persephone. She looks delicate, but this shovel'll dig you to the deepest depths of the Earth if that's where you wanna go." Bruce's voice dropped to a hushed whisper. "Is that where you're trying to go?

Hope hesitated for a bit, not knowing if "yes" was the answer he hoped to hear. She didn't want to disappoint, so she settled on a soft grunt and an ambiguous head shake.

Bruce's face relaxed into a proud smirk. He must have approved of Hope's answer. "Excellent! Let's get you rung up."

♡♡♡

At the register, Hope reflected on the $348.78 left in her bank account and assured herself the shovel wouldn't be anywhere near that price. She was wrong, of course.

"Alright, little lady. That'll be $235, even."

"Ah, ok." Hope's hands trembled as she dug through her tiny purse. *This is an investment into my future*, she thought, trying to convince herself that spending her last was a wise idea. She couldn't find her debit card in its usual places, so she moved to her pockets, then her back pocket, where she finally felt it. She let out a sigh of relief and handed it over.

"Will you be needing a bag?"

Hope shook her head.

"Makes sense! It'd be pretty awkward lugging this beauty around in a plastic bag. Would you like your receipt?"

Normally, Hope's answer to this question would be a "no", but she thought of Mrs. Choi and her insistence on a receipt for her records. "I'll take a receipt," Hope answered. "For my records."

"Your records? Of course, it's tax season! This must be a write-off for your business. Makes sense that a badass like you would own a business too."

Hope averted her eyes and nodded away Bruce's statements. He picked up on her cues and cleared the awkwardness from his throat before handing her her shovel.

"Here you go, ma'am. Thanks for shopping with us, you come back now."

"Thank you so much." Hope flashed a smile that Bruce excitedly returned.

As Hope rode home with her shiny golden shovel on her lap, she caught herself in its reflection. Although her normally neat appearance had been replaced with an unkempt bun and crooked glasses, she almost felt...pretty. For a moment, she wondered if Mona had thought the same. In the next moment, she wondered why the thought had even crossed her mind. *Someone like Mona wouldn't waste time thinking of me at all.*

"Ma'am?"

Hope looked up to see a beautiful woman turned and looking in her direction. Her smile hung on her face a bit lopsided, but in an endearing way. Her friendly eyes and deep brown skin reminded Hope of Ed.

"Me?" Hope pointed at herself, her heart fluttering in her chest.

The woman nodded. "I couldn't help but notice..." her eyes dropped from Hope's eyes to her lap, almost nervously.

Hope held her breath, and the seconds almost slowed as she waited for her response.

"...your fly's unzipped."

Hope looked down, horrified that she'd forgotten to zip up again. She nervously chuckled and tightly crossed her legs to shield the woman from the gaping hole in her jeans. "Oh, uh, thank you."

CHAPTER 15

— · —

THE FUTURIST

M ona never made it to brunch.

After pulling away from Hope's condo and sliding into the chaos of downtown traffic, she found herself stuck in a traffic jam. As she sat in her car, watching the time tick by along with the sounds of car horns and idle engines, she thought, *how weird*. She hadn't seen that coming.

It'd been years since she miscalculated a point in her future. Sometimes she'd intentionally make different choices, trying and failing to change her inevitable fate, but she'd never been *unintentionally* pushed in a different direction. In her world, there were no such things as accidents, no such things as coincidences, and no such things as surprises.

Still waiting, Mona pulled out her phone and typed "Hope Obiako" into the search bar. She wasn't a stranger to running background checks—she performed them regularly on the job. In fact, one of the first lessons she'd learned in school was how to properly research the past to make more accurate predictions of the future.

"Time is circular," Mona's Futurism professor would preach while sitting on his desk, swinging his feet back and forth like a pendulum. "The beginning is the end, and the end is the beginning. If you want to know where someone will end up, take a look at where they started."

Mona combed through Hope's beginnings and what she found was interesting but not very insightful. There was her father, Peter. A professor described as "almost frightening" and "a raging hard-to-please hothead" by his former students. She skimmed through all the feedback. She found an obscure article about Hope's high school honors project—an exploration of fairy tale subversion in modern literature that earned her a full-ride college scholarship. She bookmarked it to read later. Then, she found an old blog by an "Amber Lee", detailing college house parties and drunken nights at frat boy-infested bars. The few mentions of Hope painted her as very sober and somewhat anti-social. There was nothing in her search that could help her understand Hope's current choices. And nothing to explain Mona's own shifting future.

The 'Hope Obiako' that Mona found would never drink copious amounts of alcohol. She'd never jump in a boxing ring bare-fisted. And she'd *never* let a strange book guide her steps and obscure her future.

Traffic began to move. As Mona slowly pulled forward all she could think of was Hope, her pretty face, and her ability to change her future.

Chapter 16

The Pressure

Hope spent the rest of her afternoon digging holes in the tiny strip of grass that made up her backyard. She uncovered the bones of a small animal, a rusted hunting knife, and an impressive rock collection. But no way to eliminate her debt. She wiped the sweat from her brow and planted her golden shovel into the dirt. While punching Fear in the face was no easy task, digging her way out of debt seemed like an even more impossible feat.

Exhausted, Hope leaned against a dirt pile and looked out across the freshly exposed earth before her. For a moment, she thought of her landlady Lisa and how she'd feel seeing her property resemble an excavation site, but only for a moment.

It was nighttime when she finally gave up. The yard behind her condo was peppered with deep holes and dirt piles. Hope was covered in filth, stressed about her taxes, and was no closer to conquering her debt. She convinced herself she must be doing something wrong. Or maybe there really was nothing to be found beneath the Earth, and another delivery would come in the morning rewarding her for her tenacity.

Another delivery did not come. It didn't come the next day or the day after that, but Hope kept digging. One day there was a knock on the door, but it was only a young boy selling magazines. Hope didn't think it wise to give him any money, considering she only had one hundred and thirteen dollars to her name, but she did hand over the rock collection she'd unearthed, and he seemed pretty pleased with that. By the time Friday morning came around, Hope was, well, losing hope.

♡♡♡

Buzzzz

As Hope mentally prepared for another day of digging, she was jolted out of her thoughts by the buzzing of her cell phone.

"Hello?"

"Hope!" It was her father, Peter. "Why do you sound like that?"

"Well— "

A second voice cut into the line. "Are you sick?" It was her mother, Tochi. While her father's voice boomed, her mother's was more like a gentle song.

"I'm fine, just a bit groggy..."

"Are you not getting sleep?" Tochi asked, her voice tinged with worry.

"Ah-ah, I know you were out partying all night." Peter barked. "Party, party, party, that's all you do, *eh*?" That's literally what Hope *didn't* do, but she knew better than to contest anything her father said.

"I met one of your former students last weekend. At a networking event." Hope blurted out, hoping to steer the conversation in a different direction.

There was silence on the other line. To most, conversational silence is an awkward emptiness. A lingering space meant to fill with banter. But to Peter, silence translated to an utter lack of care. He couldn't be bothered to respond.

"He said your class was challenging." Hope continued, despite her father's indifference.

"Good. As a college course should be."

"Hope, you went to a networking event?" Tochi's excitement gently sliced through the tense atmosphere. "I'm so happy you're branching out, *ada*. I worry about how much time you spend alone. How else will you meet your husband?"

Hope's mother had been praying for a "husband from Heaven" to float down and sweep her off her feet so she could have grandchildren. Hope tried explaining her lack of interest in having children and men's lack of interest in marrying her, but when Tochi's voice cracked with sadness, she backtracked, leaving her mother hanging onto a thread of false hope.

"Yes, I did. My co-worker Alex invited me—"

"*Alex?* Is he Nigerian?" Tochi asked, an air of excitement surrounding her words.

"Well, no...he's Italian, I think."

She sucked her teeth. "You need to find Nigerian men to mingle with. Leave these White men alone."

"No, it's not like that." Hope actually wasn't sure what it was like, since she hadn't seen or heard from him since the networking event, and she was far too embarrassed to reach out herself.

"White, Black, Purple. It doesn't matter." Peter added his two cents. "You need to focus on paying off your school loans, or no one will want to marry you."

"Yes, daddy."

"Hope, have you been eating?"

"Yes, mommy." She'd been eating a diet of granola bars for weeks.

"Good. If you need me to send you anything, let me know, okay?"

"I will, but I'm fine for now." Hope lied. She knew her mother's offer was sincere, and that's what made her feel so guilty. After everything her parents sacrificed to position Hope for success, she'd failed them.

Twenty-five years prior, her parents arrived from Nigeria with nothing. Twenty-five years later, despite being thrust into a foreign land with a greatly differing culture, one lectured as a college professor at an Ivy League school, and the other saved lives as a nurse. This meant Hope was primed with the best chances to succeed in life. But twenty-five years passed, and Hope had nothing.

Time was ticking. Soon her parents would expect to see the spoils of their labor. A return on their investment in their only daughter. Then they could return to Nigeria, enjoying the rest of their days in contentment, knowing the seed they sowed together was living the life they imagined for her.

"Ok *ada*, I know you're a very busy girl. We'll let you go." Hope could feel her mother's warm smile through the phone. "Peter, won't you tell your daughter goodbye, now?

Peter grunted. That was dad-speak for "I don't care to say goodbye, I'm only doing this for your mother. Work harder and call us when you have good news".

Hope returned their goodbyes and clicked her phone to silent. No more surprise calls. It was time to get to work.

♡♡♡

Hope stood with a bandaged hand on either hip while looking out at the holes scattered across her condo's backyard. The exposed brown Earth overwhelmed what little grass was left. A huge pile of dirt, much higher than Hope was tall, sat in the corner of the yard. Her golden shovel leaned against the heap, gleaming in the sunlight.

With the burden of her parents' potential disappointment weighing on her shoulders, Hope continued to dig. The heaviness helped as she felt herself sinking deeper and deeper into the earth. Before long, the scattered holes mutated into a massive pit, with Hope at its center. She dug for hours, ignoring the pain in her fingers, the thirst in her throat, and the many missed calls from Amber. *She'll understand,* Hope thought.

Even as the sun sank into the horizon, Hope continued her dirt-riddled descent. She only stopped briefly to cough up a cloud of brown dust before continuing on into the night. Unlike washing her dishes, she was determined to see this through.

It was around eleven-thirty when Hope heard a soft *thunk* as she sunk her shovel into the ground. She used the tip of the shovel to scrape dirt off the object before stooping down and dislodging it from the soil. It was a box. A mahogany box with etched symbols that mimicked her shovel's intricate design. Hope clicked its golden latch open, expecting a box full of rare jewels or, better yet, stacks of aging cash. Instead, there was only a single rolled-up document, nicely tied with a burgundy bow. Not wanting to sully her newly found treasure, Hope snapped the box shut and began her climb back to the Earth's surface.

Hope showered until the lukewarm water turned icy cold, and even then, she continued scrubbing away the dirt until her skin felt raw. Still wrapped in a towel, she held her prize in her hands. The aging paper was tinged with yellow, and its once sharp edges curled into themselves. Hope gently released the bow and unrolled the fragile document. On the page was what appeared to be a handwritten contract. The penman was generous with his flourishes, but the terms were simple.

I, Bartholomew Livingston III, hereby grant the un-earther of this document indefinite ownership over my plot of land at 5700 Commerce Street.

Hope's hands trembled as she re-read the first sentence over and over again, questioning the validity of the document. Why would anyone do this?

You may be questioning the validity of this offer or pondering why one would do such a thing. My tale is a lengthy one, and I will not bore you with the fine details. The most pressing piece of information I have to share is that I am dying. As I lay upon my deathbed, cold and feverish and alone, I have reached the realization that I failed to make an impact on my world. Yes, to the larger world, I am a success. To the people who make up the tiny world that surrounds me daily, I am cold, displeasurable, and greedy. And I am afraid I have raised my children to be the same.

In my final acts on this Earth, I will be warm, pleasurable, and generous. I do not know who will find this contract. I do have hope that you will do great things with this modest plot of land. I will task my courier with placing it in the most opportune location, to be found at the most opportune time.

Signed Bartholomew Livingston III, on the eighteenth day of May, in the year 1870.

At the end of the contract was a line, meant to be signed in the presence of a witness.

Hope stared at the document in stunned silence for a time. Thoughts bounced around her skull as she paced around her living area, which was also her bedroom. *Is this some cruel joke? Was the Voice watching me destroy my backyard, laughing at my naivete?*

Hope had never been too interested in legal matters or history of any kind beyond what directly impacted her life in the present day. It wasn't a surprise when she scanned her bookshelf and found nothing about informal contracts *or* businessmen from the 1800's. Her subsequent internet searches yielded confusing results, and every lawyer she stumbled across charged more per hour than she currently had in the bank.

Hope sighed heavily. Another trip to the library was in order. She slipped on her sneakers and checked her cell phone, expecting another missed call from Amber. Instead, there was a single unread message from Mona:

Mona: Hey love, you crossed my mind. Let's connect soon.

Hope smiled to herself. So Mona *had* been thinking about her. She responded:

Hope: If you're free today, I'll be heading to the library in about an hour to

do some reading. I know it's not the most
interesting way to spend the afternoon,
though.

Mona responded within seconds:

Mona: I'll be there.

Mona: Send the address.

Chapter 17

—·—

The Search

Mona stood in front of the library smoking a joint when Hope arrived. Her braids were wrangled into a high ponytail, and she wore a long, sweeping skirt, flat brown sandals, and a tiny top. The rings on her fingers glistened in the sunlight.

"Hey, Hope. Didn't think I'd see you again after our one-night stand." She laughed, letting smoke escape from her teeth and nose. "You look good. How'd the digging go? Find any hidden treasure?"

Hope looked down at her dirt-covered jeans. She wasn't sure if Mona was being sincere but decided not to dwell on it. "Great, actually. I found something that might be valuable, but I've got some researching to do, hence the library," Hope smiled, "Thanks for the Kalston recommendation, by the way."

Mona studied Hope's face. Her eyes, her cheeks, her rehearsed smile. Then back to her eyes. "You're welcome," she answered in a tone Hope couldn't quite place. "You smoke?"

Hope shook her head. Mona took one more long draw before flicking the tiny joint into a nearby trash can.

"I need it for my nerves. It's been a pretty stressful week at work." Mona crossed her arms. "I hate that my time isn't my own, even on the weekends. You know?"

"I get it." Hope remembered her weekend spent toiling away on the Milton account. "Is there any way I can help?" She'd read in a book once that in a world of takers, it was *useful* people who stood out.

"This is helping. Me and my friends spend our free time sitting around one-upping each other. It's all we've got, since we're pummeled every week at work. They're at brunch right now, tearing each other apart. Gets old, fast. Trust me, I like this change of pace."

"Well," Hope looked down at her feet. "I hope I don't bore you."

"Bore me? I spend sixty hours a week fake laughing with old White men. You're a sister who spends her Friday nights punching pretentious rich kids and her Sunday afternoons at the library. You're the most interesting person I've met all week."

Hope smiled. She could feel the spark of connection growing into a small but bright, flickering flame.

"Brace yourself," Hope playfully warned as she pulled open the library doors. "Brownie Scout Troop #570 might be mounting an attack behind these doors."

Sure enough, right as the pair stepped into the library, Sofia, Lindsey, and Tasha hopped up from behind their tiny table.

"Miss! You're back! Did you bring money today?" Sofia looked up at Hope excitedly with her clipboard in hand.

Hope recoiled a bit from embarrassment. "I'm sorry, I left my money at home again."

The scouts, including Sofia, let out a collective groan.

"We'll never have enough for our trip." Sofia hung her head and slid behind the table, letting her clipboard fall to the ground. "This is my last summer before eighth grade, and I just wanted to do something meaningful on my own."

Hope wanted to tell her, *in ten years you probably won't even remember this disappointment, and if you do it will hold such little significance over the trajectory of your life that you'll simply recall the memory and shrug.* But before she could say a word, Mona knelt down in front of Sofia, who kept her head fixated on the table.

"How much do you need, sweetheart?" Mona asked.

"Three-hundred dollars."

"Do you take card?"

Sofia popped her head up. Her eyes were wet with tears. "Yes, ma'am, we do."

"Put me down for four-hundred dollars."

A huge smile spread across Sofia's face. "Thank you!" She snapped up her clipboard and took down Mona's information, then handed her a surprisingly professional-looking receipt.

The other three girls parroted Sofia's thank you's in a choir of tiny voices.

"You're welcome, darlings." Mona lovingly patted tiny Tasha, who had embraced her legs in a tight hug, on the head.

Hope watched on in awe. Mona was successful, generous, beautiful, and able to adapt to her surroundings. At least, that's how it appeared. She was everything Hope imagined a successful adult to be. Everything she wished to be. Everything she wanted.

"Have you met anyone since you moved down here?" Mona whispered from a nearby table where she sat, legs crossed, reading *Venus Fly Trap*—a book about the love life of a sentient plant.

Hope had already read it years ago and hated every page, but Mona seemed to be enjoying it well enough.

"Like, to date?" Hope sat at a computer beside her, scanning the library's database for books and news articles that mentioned Bartholemew Livingston III.

"Yeah, you dating around?"

Hope paused her search, perplexed by the tone of Mona's voice. She asked her question in a way that people do when they have a certain answer in mind, hoping you'll follow the script in their head. But Hope wasn't sure which answer would be most suitable for the current scene. Every date she'd been on since moving to the city had been a waste of time at best, and a disaster at worst.

"No, I suppose I'm just focused on my career," was the very adult response Hope settled on, but from the look on Mona's face, it was clear she went off script. "You?" she added.

Mona quickly moved on, morphing her look of disappointment into a slight smile. "You've been on that computer for a while now, need any help searching for anything?"

Hope observed Mona for a moment. She looked sincerely eager to be useful, and Hope had hit a wall, so she obliged. "Actually, I could use some help."

Mona's smile was genuine now. "Tell me what you need, and I'm on it."

"I'm looking for books or articles that mention a Bartholemew Livingston the third."

"Oh, I've heard that name before."

"You have?"

Mona nodded. "One of my boss' investors is Barry Bancroft. Bart Livingston is his wife's great-great-something or other. Left

the family with a ton of money. They're real private people, so I
don't think you'll find much here. But their future? Wild. Full of
sex scandals, bribery, bankruptcy...murder..."

"Well, that's comforting." Hope sighed and clicked out of the
database.

"Sorry, hun. What's going on?"

"I won't get into the boring details," *because they'll sound crazy,*
she thought, "but I may own a property that belonged to the Bart
Livingston. I've never procured land before, so it's kind of foreign
to me."

"Which property?"

"5700 Commerce Street, but that street only goes up to the three
hundreds."

"Well, that's because the streets downtown were reworked and
re-named over time." Mona pulled out her phone and typed into
the search bar. "According to this article, 5700 Commerce Street
in Bart Livingston's day would be, let's see. Ah, 257 Main Street
today."

Hope's heart dropped. The address Mona recited was her
former place of employment. "Th-that's the William Hensley
building."

"And William Hensley is one of our most stubborn clients.
They're not gonna just let you walk away with the deed to their
building. No matter how much it costs them."

"Of course they wouldn't." Hope laid her head in her hands.

Mona continued, "You shouldn't be at a library searching for
answers in books. You need to speak to a lawyer. A good one."
She fished through her purse before pulling out a golden business
card and handing it to Hope. "She's the best of the best. My boss

used her firm to wiggle his way out of an ironclad harassment case. Pricey, but mention me, and you might be able to work out a deal."

Hope looked down at the card. "Donna Choi?"

"Oh, so you've heard of her?"

"Yeah, we've done business in the past."

CHAPTER 18

— · —

THE LAWYER

Ladonna Seong did everything right. At least, that's what she always strived for.

She received nearly perfect marks on all her schoolwork, garnering the praise of her teachers and professors and the resentment of her peers, who shot her judgemental looks as she passed by. She ignored both. Nothing she did was for the appeasement of those around her. Every action she took served a much greater purpose, and only one opinion mattered.

When it was time to marry, Ladonna made sure to select the perfect partner that aligned with her goals—Dr. Steven Choi, a plastic surgeon. When she took his name, it elevated her social status ten-fold. She thought this was silly, of course, but that's just the way the world works. Steven paid Ladonna's way through law school, alleviating her of any burdens of debt. This was very important to her. What was also important to Ladonna was creating the perfect life so her mother could die happy and debt-free. And she did.

Ladonna would have preferred to not have children, but her mother insisted that she would find eternal happiness through the creation of life. This proved untrue for Ladonna, but she never let her mother know this, as she didn't live long enough for her to tell her. Ari Seong passed away in her sleep one day after Ki-woo Choi was born.

As Ki-woo innocently blinked up at his mother, all Ladonna could think of was her hospital bill. She knew then that babies were a never-ending time and money-suck with very little return on investment. It was at that very moment she made the decision to invest in *herself* and start her law firm, which Hope found herself walking into on a Monday morning.

Hope sat in Donna Choi's reception area, nervously awaiting her appointment, with her mahogany box sitting comfortably on her lap. She knew she needed to "dress the part", so she wore her priciest suit and her shiniest pointed-toe heels.

"I'm capable. I'm charming. People like me." Hope adjusted her glasses and repeated Dr. Marley's mantra under her breath to calm her nerves.

"Excuse me?" The receptionist looked up at Hope with impatient eyes.

"Oh, nothing, sorry."

"Hm." She resumed her typing.

Hope sat, back straight, with her legs perfectly crossed for an hour and thirty-nine minutes before she was finally summoned to see Mrs. Choi. Although her firm took up the entire floor of a luxury office building, Mrs. Choi's office was quite modest. There were no special trappings or expensive decor. Just two degrees hung above her desk, and a photo of an older woman, who Hope thought resembled her a bit.

"Hello, Ms. Oh-bee-ahko, please have a seat."

Hope sat across from Mrs. Choi, minding her posture and trying her best to maintain eye contact. "Hello, Mrs. Choi. I hope you and Ki-woo have been well?"

Mrs. Choi tensed a bit at the mention of her son. Hope felt the shift and settled back into her chair.

"Ki-woo is just fine. He abandoned your briefcase only an hour after we left the park." Her face softened. "But I was happy to be relieved from his cries, even for a moment."

Mrs. Choi laced her fingers together on her desk and leaned forward. "I normally only meet face-to-face with clients who have already paid for my time, but since we've done prior business, I'm bending my rules a bit. You mentioned a contract?"

"Yes." Hope placed her box on the desk. "I found this buried in my backyard."

Mrs. Choi opened the box and carefully unraveled the aged contract. Time ticked on as she silently read through the document, before she finally spoke, "I see."

"Well?" Hope leaned forward excitedly.

"I'll have my team verify the validity of this document, but if this is legitimate, then you could potentially be the owner of a commercial property worth multi-millions."

Hope blinked in disbelief. She clutched the sides of her chair to calm herself. "So I'd really own the William Hensley building?"

Mrs. Choi nodded. "As the maxim goes, 'For whoever owns the soil, it is theirs up to heaven...and down to hell.'" She pointed downward to emphasize the word *hell*. "But the biggest hurdle will be battling whoever owned this property up until the moment you found this contract. I assume they'll be putting up a fight." Hope could have sworn the corners of Donna's mouth lifted into a slight smile, but only for a moment.

"A fight?"

"Now, let's talk payment. No offense Hope, but I know you can't afford me."

Hope nodded her head. She couldn't be offended because it was true. "My friend Mona Kitt mentioned you might be able to work out a deal for me? She's a Futurist at Kline Turner."

"I do know Mona. I've worked closely with her firm." Donna tapped her pen on her desk and looked down in thought before continuing, "I don't enjoy investing my time into things that don't yield results. I don't take cases I know I can't win. And I don't take on clients who I know can't pay. But," she leaned back in her chair, "if this document is valid, this could be a life-changing case for the both of us."

"If it's true, if I'll really be a multi-millionaire, I'll definitely pay you then, Mrs. Choi. You have my word."

Mrs. Choi eyed Hope as one would examine a jug of milk with a curious odor. After a few tense seconds, she nodded. "Alright, then. I'll have a contract drawn up, outlining your debt to me."

CHAPTER 19

— · —

THE LANDLORD

O n a high after her meeting with Mrs. Choi, Hope floated
home, thinking of all the ways she could use her future
multi-millions. She'd pay off her student loans first, of course, then
she'd buy a home for her parents in Nigeria. Maybe even utilize
her faded orange book and start a business. She'd have the time,
resources, and money available, so why not? She could finally write
a novel and travel the world, signing copies at bookstores in faraway
places. She made a mental note to call Mona to share the good
news. But first, she needed to relish in the win.

By the time Hope's excitement dropped her ever-so-gently at the
front steps of her condo, she was a bit disturbed to find her door
slightly ajar. She hadn't remembered leaving the door unlocked, let
alone cracked open, but she also hadn't been herself lately.

She hesitated for a moment, imagining thieves rummaging
through her belongings, finding nothing of value, then waiting
for her arrival so they could taunt the poor soul who lived
in such bedraggled conditions. After a few seconds, she settled
on the unlocked door simply being a symptom of her own
absentmindedness. She pushed the door open, fully expecting to
be greeted by her worn-down accommodations, but Hope was

more than surprised to find her landlord Lisa sitting, arms crossed, on her couch-bed.

Lisa was a tiny firecracker of a woman. Retired with no children, but with an enormous amount of money from her second divorce, Lisa had a taste for oversized palm tree printed shirts. There were exactly forty-seven of them, in various shades of ombre, hanging in her closet. She never smiled but still had a vibrant spirit. At that very moment, though, that vibrancy was nowhere to be found. Lisa's deep wrinkles carved cavernous frown lines into her face, and her thin dark eyebrows were twisted into a look of disgust. Her cropped jet-black hair almost stood on end. She was furious.

"L-lisa?"

"I thought you were on a business trip, Hope?"

"I was, I've just returned." Hope did look very business-like, and if she weren't shaking in her boots, she would have been extremely proud of herself.

"Liar," Lisa scoffed. "Imagine my surprise when I called your "job", and a woman named Monica informed me you were fired."

Hope's ears warmed with embarrassment. "She's not allowed to disclose that."

"Does it matter? She told the truth. You lied. And the worst of all? You've destroyed my property."

"I'm sorry Lisa, but—"

"Sorry isn't enough. You've yet to pay your rent on time, and I can't risk any further damage to my property. Be out by the end of the week."

"But Lisa, no one could possibly want this place in the state that it's in. Just give me a little more time. Please. I swear I'll be able to fix everything. I'll be able to pay you soon."

"No, I've heard that a million times. I want you out. If you're not gone by next Sunday, I'll be calling the police." Lisa stood to her feet, adding, "and I still want my rent money!" before blowing out of Hope's, well technically her own, front door in a dramatic fashion, letting it slam behind her.

Hope fell to her knees in a panic and slid *How to Be a Better Adult* from its hiding place under her couch-bed, her hands shaking ever so slightly as she opened it to reveal its next chapter. The pages were still blank.

"No, no, no." Hope flipped through more pages, each one taunting her with its vast emptiness. "Voice?" her own voice cracked as she called out to no one. "Voice! P-please, come back. I did what you wanted. Why is this happening to me?"

Hope pulled her faded orange book from her bookshelf, flipping to page fifty-seven. She bypassed the advice on how to be likable, instead hoping to find an ominous, all-knowing message. There was nothing on the page that wasn't there before. She threw the book to the ground, then fell to the ground herself in defeat.

Hope's heart pounded in her chest, and warm tears blurred her vision. Her mind raced, attempting to make sense of her predicament. She sifted through scenario after scenario, choice after choice, around and around, and the only conclusion she came to, no matter where she started or where she ended, was that she was fundamentally flawed. Broken. A self-saboteur incapable of successfully existing in the world. An *aspiring* adult. But never a seasoned professional.

"I don't understand any of this." She quietly cried to herself.

In twenty-five years, she'd achieved nothing of note. And in twenty-five more, who's to say how much further she would sink? Like Mona, Hope peered into her future and saw absolutely nothing. Only a gaping black hole. But that vision of nothingness that had once confused and disappointed her suddenly morphed into something light and warm and...*absolute.*

That warm feeling embraced Hope like an old friend, promising her reprieve and offering her answers in the midst of confusion. The feeling lifted her off the ground and led her to the bathroom. There, the feeling opened her medicine cabinet, revealing a perfect row of over-the-counter drugs. Hope opened each bottle, one at a time, and emptied their contents into her palm until she couldn't hold anymore. She thought she ought to leave a note, a bit of a send-off to the world, but as soon as the thought came, it went.

Knowing the "why" wouldn't matter to anyone anyway. And she was certain they'd take one look at her piteous legacy and think, "I understand. Poor thing. Surprising she didn't pull the trigger sooner". Hope lifted the handful of pills to her lips, fully prepared to swallow them all.

But then there was a knock at the door.

It was a faint knock. Almost as if the person wasn't sure they were at the correct residence but thought, 'ah, might as well give it a shot'. Hope gently poured the pills into her makeup bag to recover later, and hesitantly answered the door.

Fully expecting to find her fuming landlord returning back to berate her further, Hope was all the more startled to see her best friend Amber standing at her doorstep. She had a slightly confused look on her face and was holding a small white box in one hand and a six-pack of beer in the other.

CHAPTER 20

THE QUESTION

Hope hadn't seen her friend in over a year and was taken aback by not only her presence but also her appearance. Amber was never the type to wear flashy clothing, always opting to hide her loud personality under thrifted band t-shirts artfully tucked into oversized mom jeans. But there she stood draped in an expensive-looking, curve-hugging dress and pointed heels. Her previously shoulder-length curls were dyed a coppery red and cropped into a short, tapered style. She also sported a new pair of bold black cat-eye glasses, the kind that trendy interior designers wore on magazine covers.

"Amber?"

"Hope?" Amber also examined Hope's changes, taking in her tear-stained face, rumpled clothing, and pained expression. "You ok? Your job still stressing you out?"

Hope nervously chuckled, racking her brain for a proper response.

"No, I actually just quit....today. It was tough and pretty awkward, but you know I hated that place."

Amber's face softened into what Hope recognized as relief.

"Girl, I understand how that feels. I'm happy to hear you quit that terrible job. You deserve better."

"Yeah, it was for the best," Hope slid out of her front door, shutting it behind her to shield Amber from the sight of her gaudy chartreuse walls and musky carpet. "But what are you doing down here? I'm so happy to see you! "

"I've been trying to call you, girl! I was gonna mail this like I do everything else," Amber motioned towards the box in her hands, "But, I don't know, I just needed to see you. I really should've come to see you a long time ago. I guess life just got in the way." She smiled, "Mind if I come inside?"

"It's such a mess in there. I'd hate for you to see my place when it's not at its best."

Amber shook her head and laughed.

"Hope, are you forgetting that nasty dorm we lived in? You know I've seen it all."

Amber reached behind Hope and turned the doorknob quicker than she could stop her, exposing her dirt-covered condo, disheveled couch-bed, and sink full of unwashed dishes. Hope's heart sank as she watched the smile fade from Amber's face, revealing a deep look of concern.

"Ok...what's going on?".

Amber sat on Hope's couch bed, cradling the small white box in her arms, as Hope spun a tall tale of quitting her overbearing job and throwing herself into new hobbies, like gardening, to pass the time while on her much-needed break from the overwhelm of corporate America. She lied that her bright green walls and unfortunate plumbing were simply part of a "renovation project"

that went hilariously wrong. And that the dishes were leftover from a group of contractors who devoured the contents of her fridge as Hope awkwardly watched on, too anxious to speak up and stop them.

Amber listened, quietly, processing Hope's every fabricated word until she was done. Then, she laughed. Hope nervously chuckled along as tears of amusement streamed down Amber's face.

"You're so crazy Hope, I love it. You're really living down here!"

"Yeah, heh, I'm definitely living. So, what's new with you?"

"Well, I wanted to ask you something." Amber wiped her tears and handed Hope the box. "We've known each other for six years now, and I'm so happy to call you my best friend. And I can't imagine doing anything major without you right by my side and, well, go ahead you can open it."

Hope opened the box, revealing a card and an even smaller box. Inside *that* box was a small, leather-bound journal with the words "A Journal For Hope" embossed in gold, flourishing letters on its cover.

"Wow, Amber, this is beautiful".

"Isn't it? I bought it off an old lady at the flea market. You know I love my thrifted finds, girl. I thought it was so funny it already had your name on it."

"I love it so much, thank you!"

"Ok, now, read the card!"

Hope, ever obedient, did as she was told. The small white card was nearly blank, minus the tiny gold letters printed in the middle. Hope had to squint as she read the words: *Will you be my maid of honor*?

A warm smile spread across Hope's face. "Amber? Are you serious? Jimoh finally proposed?"

Amber excitedly nodded, her tears of laughter morphing into tears of joy. "It was beautiful. There were roses and candles everywhere. The most romantic setup I could've ever imagined."

Hope tried to recall the most romantic gesture she'd ever experienced, but she couldn't. Every almost-relationship Hope found herself entangled in was steeped in awkwardness and miscommunication. There were no signs of the kind of heart-fluttering romance she'd read about in books. She had convinced herself that those grand gestures didn't happen in real life. But here was Amber proving it was possible, just not for Hope. She remembered the pills in her makeup bag.

"So, will you be my maid of honor?" Amber smiled widely.

"Well, I—" Hope tucked away the tiny pang of jealousy that threatened to eclipse her genuine excitement for her friend. "Of course I will."

"Oh, Hope, you have no idea how happy I am!"

"I bet! When's the wedding?"

"This fall, in Ibiza. And all the bridesmaids will be wearing red, of course. Let me show you the dresses." Amber pulled up a photo on her cell phone of a silky blood-red gown. As she explained how she found the perfect dress, Hope couldn't help but notice the price listed right below. Four-hundred and twenty-nine dollars. Her heart sank as she tried her best to maintain the smile pasted on her face.

"It's a beautiful dress but—"

"I can't wait to see you in it." Amber leaned over, releasing two cans of beer from their plastic trappings and handing one to Hope.

"I know you don't like drinking like that, but I was hoping to drag you out to the club and celebrate like old times. I miss our college days. Life is so stressful now, you know?"

Hope nodded in agreement and took the beer. Life was indeed stressful, which is why she had every intention of escaping it.

Amber cracked hers open, smiling from ear to ear. "Cheers to new beginnings?"

Hope raised her own can, "And endings."

CHAPTER 21

— · —

THE CLUB

Hope didn't want to go out that evening. She sighed as she slid into a slinky dress and strappy heels. When she slicked her hair into a classy low bun, it was the last thing she felt like doing. But as she maneuvered around the handful of pills in her makeup bag, fishing out her mascara to complete her look, she caught a glimpse of Amber quietly scanning her bookshelf.

Amber wasn't much of a reader. She preferred to indulge in more physically exhaustive hobbies like hiking, kickboxing, and running. She wasn't admiring the new titles or taking note of which books she'd like to read. Hope knew her friend was scanning her bookshelf to understand what was missing so she could fill the gaps.

Amber had always been the type of friend to notice Hope's gaps. Whenever she felt lonely on campus, Amber would show up, almost instinctively, with drinks and board games in hand to bring a smile to her face. When she experienced her first heartbreak, Amber delivered flowers to remind her she was loved by someone—even if it wasn't the person she'd been pining for. And now, somehow, Amber knew Hope was missing something. Something even Hope herself couldn't figure out.

Amber turned, meeting Hope's eye. She looked pensive, as if she had something profound to say. Her gaze lingered on Hope for a bit before she finally spoke, "Can I use the bathroom before we head out?"

"Oh, uh, of course."

Later that night, Hope and Amber hopped from upscale club to upscale club, funded by Jimoh's credit card because, apparently, he received travel points with every swipe. Hope made every effort to stay sober despite Amber's every effort to end the night in a drunken stupor together. As their night wore on, Hope switched her own shots of vodka with water and slyly asked each bartender for pineapple juice instead of the fruity mixed drinks Amber *thought* she was ordering for the two of them. By the time they reached the third bar, Amber was tripping over her words and her feet, weighed down by a considerable amount of alcohol. A very sober Hope held her steady.

"Not to sound dramatic and completely unhinged, but I'd commit heinous crimes for you. Like, *really* bad ones." Amber's words slurred into a singular stream of vowels, nouns, and adjectives. "That's how much I love you."

"I love you, too. But I'm not sure about the heinous crimes." Hope laughed.

"I miss you!" Amber embraced Hope. "*Please* come live with me. Jimoh and I are closing on a house soon. I know you, and I know you'll say no, but there's plenty of space, I swear."

Another weed of jealousy twisted up through Hope's chest. "You bought a house?"

Amber nodded as she struggled to take a seat at the bar. "Jimoh's parents helped us with the down payment. It's nice, but it's, it's so far away from everything and so *permanent*. Honestly, none of this feels real or even right. I don't know if I wanna do any of this."

Amber hung her head with what Hope recognized as sorrow, but to everyone else, she must have appeared too intoxicated to hold her head up on her own.

"I understand that feeling," Hope assured her friend. "But a house, a ring, a wedding. Those are all great things. Everything according to plan, right?"

Amber shrugged. "Whose plan, though? I feel like I'm just following a script that I didn't even write."

Hope's ears perked up. "Wait, what do you mean by that?"

"Never mind, I should be grateful, right?" Amber lifted her head, her eyes glossed over with intoxication and sadness. "Hope, there's a creepy man staring at the back of your head."

Hope turned to follow Amber's gaze. To her dismay, she found herself face to face with Alex, with only a single barstool standing between them and several empty glasses scattered across the bar before him. A slender older woman sat beside him, her legs wrapped around his waist like a spider, and her arms draped around his shoulders. Her greying hair was hoisted into a messy bun atop her head, and remnants of her bright red lipstick made faint appearances on Alex's lips as she continued to kiss his neck and face. There were no traces of his normally pleasant demeanor. Instead, he stared back at Hope with bloodshot eyes and a blank, robotic expression.

"Seems we can't escape each other, can we?" he hissed.

"Oh, uh, hey, Alex." Hope nervously shifted on her stool. "Don't worry, I'm sober this time. So no punching, I promise." Hope chuckled. Alex remained stoic. "Sorry," Hope added to diffuse the awkwardness.

"Alex? *This* is the Alex that was taking you out to lunch?" Amber, oblivious to the awkwardness of the situation, leaned forward, hoping to be introduced.

"Yup," Hope winced with embarrassment remembering how that lunch, and her naivete, led to her termination.

"Oh, she told you about that?" Alex scoffed, taking a swig of the drink in front of him. "Did she also tell you how her drunken antics got me banned from a prestigious networking group?"

The older woman stopped kissing Alex's face and shot Hope a steely cold look. "It's ok baby, my husband'll get you back in. I'll make sure of it."

"Thanks, Angie," Alex responded without taking his eyes off Hope.

"You were *banned*?" Hope shrank in her seat, avoiding Alex and Angie's dual stares.

"Drunken antics? Hope, what happened?" Amber asked.

"I invited her out, hoping she'd have some, I dunno, decorum? Instead, she knocked out the son of a Fortune-500 CEO." Alex rolled his eyes and fixed his gaze back on Hope.

"Sorry, Alex," Hope's cheeks burned with embarrassment, and tears rushed to blur her vision.

"Whatever. I consider it a challenge. I'm already working on a way back in with Angie here," Alex turned and pecked Angie on the cheek as she squealed like a schoolgirl, "and a couple more nights with Monica and I'll be working on the seventh floor. All according to plan."

Hope blinked back her tears as a realization slowly crept through her brain. "You slept with Monica?"

"I'm sleep-*ing* with Monica. And she's made an invaluable contribution to my career trajectory."

Hope glanced at an unaffected Angie as she continued planting kisses on the side of Alex's face.

"Did you know she'd have me fired?"

"Fired? You told me you quit..." A confused Amber interjected.

"I knew she wanted you gone." Alex shrugged. "She said your personality annoyed her or something. I just rode on the coattails of your inevitable departure." He took another sip of his drink, "I did try to help you out, though."

A volcanic eruption of anger burned through Hope's chest, setting ablaze the feelings of guilt and jealousy she'd been harboring all evening. The heat of her anger culminated at her fists, which she clenched so hard she shook. *Don't punch him*, she thought. *Don't make a scene. Don't punch him*, she repeated in her mind, unsuccessfully fighting against her now natural instinct to strike annoying men.

"Hope, you're shaking. You alright?" Amber's intoxication seemed to fade as her concern for her friend grew.

Hope unclenched her fists and closed her eyes to calm herself. She inhaled and exhaled, thinking of all the proper, adult ways to express her disappointment and anger. But before she could connect her mind to her mouth, a stream of words came tumbling out.

"You know, I used to think so highly of you at work. But you're actually pathetic. You manipulated me. And you thrive on using people to feed your ego."

"Hope!" Amber gasped, her drunken face beaming with pride.

Hope gasped as well. She couldn't believe the words that had just escaped her lips.

"Alex, I'm-I'm sorry." Hope stepped back, shocked at her own cruelty

"Manipulated *you*?" Alex laughed. "Oh please, you're an adult. I offered you a favor. You accepted it. Simple as that."

"B-but you knew I'd be fired—"

"And I said you were on the chopping block, didn't I? And you were happy to accept the help. In fact, I've done nothing but help you out. What exactly have I gotten in return?"

"Well—" Hope thought for a moment. She knew in her heart that Alex was being unreasonable or unfair, or unkind, but her mind just couldn't make sense of it. Logically, he was right. He did warn her about being "on the chopping block". He did complete her impossible project. And he did invite her to an exclusive networking event.

"I suppose I do owe you..."

"I know one way you could pay me back." A smile spread across Alex's face as his eyes flicked up and down, taking in Hope's physique in her tight dress, "And if all goes well, maybe I can get you your job back."

Hope crossed her arms to shield her body from Alex's violating stare. Her cheeks burned with embarrassment. "What are you—"

Before she could say anymore, Amber grabbed her hand. "Absolutely not. Fuck this guy. You don't owe him anything. Let's go."

Alex continued on as Amber dragged Hope away, "Let me know when you're ready to be the grown woman you are." He winked.

"I can't believe *that* was Alex!" Amber called out as the pair navigated away from the bar through a dark sea of strobe lights, spilled drinks, and sweaty bodies.

"Me neither! I've never seen him like this!" Hope shouted back, still reeling from their encounter.

"Hope?" A wobbly Amber turned, clutching Hope's shoulders in her hands to steady herself.

"Hm?"

"Mind taking me back to my hotel? I think, I think I'm gonna puke!"

CHAPTER 22

— • —

THE PROMISE

"I've got about twenty minutes before I need to leave for the airport. My flight's at seven-thirty." In the morning, Amber checked her watch while meticulously packing her belongings into her designer luggage.

With her tailored suit jacket and swift, purposeful movements, no one would have known she spent the entire night heaving over a toilet. Her bounce-back from a night of drinking had always been impressive in college, but this was awe-inspiring to Hope, who sat on Amber's hotel bed, peeking out from her blankets with slightly smeared eyeliner and a single strap of her dress hanging from her shoulders.

"Need help with anything?" Hope asked, wiping the sleep from her eyes.

"No, it's alright. You should probably relax. You had a lot to drink last night."

"You're right." She was wrong, of course, but Amber didn't need to know that. It was much easier to blame the events of the evening on intoxication. "You still feeling overwhelmed?"

Amber paused her packing. "I don't know why I complained. I'm sorry, I really should be grateful. Jimoh and I have our issues, but he's a good guy."

Hope shook her head, "It's ok to complain. Nothing ever feels as good as it looks before you get there."

"Speaking of such, why didn't you tell me you were fired? And that sleazy Alex guy...I can't believe you've been dealing with this all on your own."

"I was embarrassed. I'm still embarrassed. I had an opportunity people would kill for, and I fumbled it."

"Maybe I was a little too drunk, but it sounded like none of that was your fault."

"Doesn't matter. I'm a failure either way." Hope thought of Mona. "Maybe if I were more likable, more...professional, these things wouldn't happen to me."

"You've always been so concerned about that, but you're more than likable, Hope. I wish you knew that. People are just...disappointing." Amber sat on the bed beside Hope, laying a comforting hand on her shoulder.

"Saying people are disappointing means nothing. Yeah, they're horrible, but *I'm* the one who ends up hurt in the end. So does it even matter? Something's clearly wrong with me."

"Why are you *so* hard on yourself? Ok, the job didn't work out. You can get another one. But at least you can always say you *tried*." Amber sighed, "Maybe one day I'll have the courage to do the same. I just smile and do what's expected of me. My mind tells me it's easier that way. But it's...suffocating."

It dawned on Hope that despite earning every badge of adulthood available to her thus far, Amber felt just as dissatisfied as she did. Just as stifled by the expectations of some faceless council appointed to deem one suitable enough to hold the title of "successful adult". So, she gave her friend the absolute best advice that she could.

"Maybe you should try punching fear in the face."

"Punching *what*?"

"The thing that scares you most. Whatever's standing in the way of you and freedom. Maybe you'll regret it. Maybe you won't, but at least you'll feel something. At least you would've tried, right?"

Amber thought for a moment. "You're right. I need to do something totally out of my comfort zone." She stood and zipped up her suitcase. "You know what? I know exactly what I need to do."

"What is it?" Hope imagined Amber throwing caution to the wind and moving out West to live the carefree life she'd always dreamed of.

"Have a baby."

"A...*baby?*"

"Maybe all I need to fill the void is a child. Jimoh's been talking about wanting kids for ages, and I've just been so uninterested. *But* maybe that's the fear I need to face and—"

Hope nodded along as Amber described the typical life of a married woman. Taking her kid to school, to their piano recitals, and to sporting events. She fantasized about folding clothes, changing diapers, and bickering with Jimoh. As she spoke, the chasm between them grew larger and larger. Hope finally accepted what she knew from the moment she saw Amber standing on her doorstep. That on the path of maturity Amber had outpaced her entirely. Even if she felt the same frustrations as Hope, she was better equipped with the tools to succeed. She knew the script, and whether she liked it or not, she was able to follow it.

" —anyway, I'll keep you posted on my prenatal journey. And of course, if you need us to cover your dress for the wedding you can absolutely let me know and we'll take care of it, ok?"

Hope nodded.

"Feel free to stay here until check out. I called to extend your stay 'til one since I know you like to sleep in after a night out."

"Thanks, Amber."

"Hope," Amber turned to face Hope. She flashed a warm smile, "I'll miss you."

Hope returned Amber's smile. "I'll miss you too."

The two embraced, but as Hope tried pulling away, Amber leaned in closer and whispered in her ear. "I noticed the empty pill bottles in your bathroom. I know things are tough right now, but I *can't* lose my best friend. Don't do that to me."

Amber released Hope from her embrace, revealing downturned eyes tinged with sadness.

"I, I won't. I promise." Hope stammered, taken aback.

"Thank you, Hope. Please call me if you need me." Amber quickly replaced the despair on her face with her usual smile before rolling her luggage to the door. "Girl, I forreal better get going before I miss my flight and Jimoh loses his mind. I'll see you in a few months at the wedding rehearsal!"

And just like that, she was gone. Hope wrapped herself in the hotel comforter and fell back onto the bed, deeply sighing on the way down. As she laid there on her back, her loneliness returned, heavy as ever.

While the reality of her life properly settled in, the last thing Hope wanted to be was alive. What a burden it was to breathe and make choices. All day. Every day. With each choice having the capability to completely ruin your future. Hope wanted nothing more than to escape, but succumbing to the bright, warm, absolute meant potentially ruining her best friend's wedding. And *that* she couldn't do.

CHAPTER 23

—·—

THE STORAGE SPACE

I n the days that followed Amber's visit, Hope did a number of things—none of which included taking the pills in her makeup bag. As tempting as they were, any thought of the bright warm absolute that the pills would have afforded her was drowned out by the sound of Amber's voice. *Don't do that to me*, replaced *you have no future* as the thought that ran laps around Hope's skull. She couldn't attend her friend's wedding if she were dead, so she postponed the plan. Instead, with only a few days left to vacate her condo, she listed her belongings for sale online.

The first piece of furniture to go was Hope's couch-bed, sold to a trio of art school students moving into their first apartment together.

"The worn and torn look is *all* the rage in the modern interior design space," said the tallest of the three as he knelt down to examine the couch-bed's weak seams and dusty underbelly.

The next tallest stated how "the state of this ragged resting space speaks to capitalism's brutal beatdown of the middle class". The shortest just rested his chin between his thumb and forefinger and quietly nodded. They offered Hope fifty dollars, and she accepted.

Next to go was her golden shovel, sold to a lanky, pale man with alarmingly long fingers and a mischievous grin. When Hope jokingly mentioned the shovel could dig him to the center of the Earth, the man's face darkened as he stoically answered, "I know." He handed Hope two hundred dollars and left without saying another word.

An hour later, an aging woman with a crook in her neck took a special interest in Hope's dirty dishes, but she couldn't bring herself to sell them, so she gave them away for free. The woman was beside herself with gratitude.

"Thank you, young lady," she croaked, while cradling a crusty plate to her chest. "You have no idea what this means to me."

"Erm, you're welcome?"

"You'll be blessed beyond what you can imagine. Good fortune will soon come your way. I'm sure of it."

"Oh, ok. Thanks." Hope answered while walking towards the door, hoping to will the woman away from her space.

In between sales, Hope made calls to Donna Choi. Each one, but one, went unanswered. When she did reach Donna's receptionist, she informed Hope that the firm was slammed with clients and promised they would find time to work on her case.

"The law, like a child, tends to crawl on," she added. Hope hadn't expected to hear much more than that.

After three days, she'd sold most of her belongings, minus her bookshelf, and earned around four-hundred and thirty-one dollars, enough to hire movers and secure a storage unit for a month.

♡♡♡

Hope's storage unit was much smaller than her condo but felt, surprisingly, more inviting. The cold metal and hard concrete floor were a step up from her loud chartreuse walls and curiously-scented carpet. Since there was no sink, there were no dirty dishes. And without a bathroom, the faulty plumbing that plagued her last place of dwelling was no longer an issue. The only problems were the stale, cold air and lack of sunlight. And she did miss her couch-bed. Instead, she laid on the floor and wrapped herself in a thick blanket.

It was her bookshelf that really tied it all together, making her feel as at-home as possible. She felt insulated from the outside world. Shielded from things like rent payments, corporate jargon, and sky-high expectations. In her storage unit, she could just be.

But that feeling of contentment didn't last long. After two weeks of consuming nothing but granola bars, lying about her well-being to Amber, dodging her parents, and ignoring Mona's calls, a realization hit Hope. With only two more weeks left to come up with her next month's storage fee, she had no way of paying.

Bzzzzz.

Hope fished her buzzing cell phone from the folds of her blanket and watched an unknown number flash across its screen. She imagined it to be a debt collector. But she was so desperate to escape her thoughts, that she answered anyway.

"Hello?"

"Is this Hope Oh-bee-awko?"

Hope recognized this voice. It was Donna Choi.

"Mrs. Choi?"

"Is this Hope? Yes, or no?"

"Er, yes, sorry, it's Hope. What's up?"

"I don't have much time to spare. As you can imagine, I'm a very busy woman."

"But...you called me?"

"And you're lucky I did. Why didn't you tell me about your *Sports Illuminated* feature? I read it, and so did the W&H lawyers."

"Ok, so did they want an autograph or something?" Hope remembered she'd actually never read the article but, apparently, it was awe-inspiring and impressive enough to be hung in the Kalston's break room as motivation.

"An autograph? Hope, they're saying you're unhinged. A scorned employee, prone to violent outbursts. Did you punch Nick Loeser? At a networking event?"

Hope's heart sank, "I, I did but—"

"And did you breach the terms of your employment by sharing confidential files?"

"Yes, but I was manipulated."

"And did you verbally assault an 'Alexander Rossi' at a 'Euphoria Nightclub'?"

"Really? He's saying I *assaulted* him? He's the one who got me fired."

Donna sighed. "Ok. I'll figure something out. It'll take a while. As you may have heard, the law—"

"Tends to crawl on. Yes, I've heard." Hope reflected on the two weeks left on her lease. "What does the timeline look like?"

"With the way their team is fighting back, this will take at least two years. But probably five."

"Ok, thanks, Mrs. Choi." Hope hung up. She didn't reflect on anything she'd just heard as, to her, none of it was real. Two years was just twenty-four months too late, with an outcome nestled in a future that she couldn't fathom anyway. Instead of reflecting on things she had no sense of, she decided to do all she could in the moment and find a job.

"Your resume, well, it's really impressive—" Hope sat across from Bruce, in the Kalston's breakroom, as he flipped through her printed work history. Unlike the smiling, helpful version of him she'd met on the store floor, as an interviewer Bruce was serious and a bit terse, but only in the same way a child is when imitating their least favorite parent. "—but it looks like you don't have a current address?"

"No, I don't currently have an address." Hope looked past Bruce at the photo of herself thumbtacked on the store's colorful bulletin board. It was a page ripped from her *Sports Illuminated* feature, with the headline "Where there's a will, there's Hope".

"I'm sorry to tell you this," Bruce sighed, "I'd hire you in a heartbeat if I could but—"

"I need a permanent address."

"You need a permanent address," Bruce confirmed. "For our paperwork. And honestly, for any job around here. I'm sorry, Hope. But a bigshot like you? You won't be down and out for long. Where there's a will, there's Hope, right?" He flashed a smile while jabbing at the air.

"Right." Hope smiled back, just to keep Bruce's own hope alive.

♡♡♡

After her interview, Hope decided to treat herself to an individual-sized bottle of tequila. Of course, she despised the taste of tequila, and any alcohol really, but when one is backed against a wall with all options exhausted, a person tends to act in ways they normally wouldn't.

The cashier at *Quick Serve*, a corner store by Hope's storage unit, stared blankly over the register waiting for Hope to finish rummaging through her embarrassingly empty purse so she could purchase her alcohol and he could end his shift.

"How much was it again?" she asked, stalling for time as she counted the quarters that lined the bottom of her bag.

"Three dollars, even." He responded, blinking slowly.

"Ah, here you go," Hope slid a battered dollar bill and eight quarters across the counter. She could have used her debit card, but she had exactly fifty-seven dollars in her bank account, and she had to make it stretch, just in case. "I figured I might as well use up the change in my purse, you know?"

"Right. Thanks." The cashier plopped the money into the register without counting and handed Hope her bottle of liquid gold.

Back at her storage unit, nestled in her cocoon of a blanket, Hope began to drink. She played a game with herself, taking a sip of tequila any time she laughed at a poorly written line of text in *Taking of the Rose*. After five pages, she was quite drunk.

The sight of a young woman drunkenly reading on the concrete floor of a storage unit after losing almost everything she placed value in might have raised a few flags of concern to the average person. Maybe they'd think she had spiraled, or had reached rock bottom, or had lost her will to live. And those things were all true, however, this was part of her plan. Hope may have felt numb, empty, and defeated. But the last thing she wanted to feel was alone.

After the alcohol properly settled into her bloodstream, she called out, "Voice?"

There were a few empty moments of silence before she heard an answer.

Hope? The Voice was faint, like it had been woken from a deep sleep. *I see you've been drinking again.* The Voice yawned.

"I figured I could reach you if I lowered my inhibitions."

I see. Did you need something?

"Yes, I mean, no, I, erm." Hope rocked off of her side and sat up in her blanket cocoon. "I guess I just wanted to talk to someone."

There was another pause before the voice responded.

Oh, ok. Well, I'm more of an ominous, all-knowing kind of voice, but I suppose I can chat. What's going on?

"You've been a bit less foreboding, honestly, but that's beside the point. In your absence, I realized I didn't consider how lonely you must feel in there."

"Interesting."

"So, I just wanted to learn more about you. Who are you?"

I can't answer that, Hope.

"Ok, I won't press the issue," Hope wanted so badly to press the issue, but she'd read in a book that boundaries, no matter how firm, should always be respected. "Do you have any hobbies, by the way? Any fun things that light your soul on fire?" Hope paused. "If you have a soul, that is."

I'm actually partial to baking. If I weren't currently in your mind, I'd probably be somewhere decorating cookies.

"Everyone seems to have some kind of escape from the madness, right?"

The Voice was quiet, but Hope imagined it was nodding.

"Voice?" Tears welled in Hope's eyes as she spoke. "Do you know anything about a bright, warm, absolute feeling?"

Yes, the feeling of death.

"If I died, would you be ok? Would you find another mind to inhabit? Or would it end your life too?"

You've been thinking about death quite a bit, haven't you?

"Please answer. I need to know. Life is just...it's just too hard."

There was a pause, and Hope imagined the voice was thinking. Finally, it spoke. *This isn't how I imagined this to go. How'd this stray so far from the plot?* Hope could have sworn she heard the sound of pages flipping.

"Because I'm clearly incapable of doing anything right. Even when the answers are spelled out for me and—the plot?"

Hm?

"You just said this strayed from the plot. What plot?"

Dunno, I'm just a voice in your head.

"Are you—you're the one writing *How To Be a Better Adult*?"

What are you talking about?

"No, the book doesn't have a *plot*." Hope unwrapped herself and drunkenly stood to her feet. "You must be writing about...*me*?"

Hope, you've been drinking.

"I'm not losing my mind," Hope was pacing now, her mind sorting through all her feelings of life feeling out of her control. The book, the firing, the unfortunate series of events that led her to this very moment. "I'm just not in full control of it. My life's being authored by a sadistic asshole."

Sadistic? No, I'm just writing what I know—

"Ah ha! I knew it. I knew it!"

The Voice sighed.

Ok, fine. Hope heard the sound of a chair groaning under the weight of the Voice's frustration. *I've been drafting your story for years now, but I keep pushing up against a wall. I had to take a break, to clear the writer's block. I didn't know I'd come back to...this.*

Hope stopped her pacing and leaned against her bookshelf, crossing her arms in frustration.

"Why couldn't you just write me differently? More charming. More cunning?"

Because, the Voice sighed, *because you're a representation of me. My personality, my fears, and my failures. And I can't just snap my fingers and make myself more charming, can I?*

"So instead, you drop a strange book on my doorstep? Like that isn't more farfetched..."

All I ever wanted was an Adult Handbook. Something to navigate my world with. So I gave you one. And things, they just, well, they seem to have gotten out of hand.

"Yeah, no kidding. Who are you, exactly?"

I can't—

"I deserve to know."

The Voice paused for a few moments before answering, *You wouldn't know, even if I told you.*

"Ok, whatever. So how does all this end? How long will the law "crawl on"? Will I ever get a happy ending?"

I—I don't know. I've just been letting my intuition guide me to the perfect ending, and now...I think I've lost the plot.

"Well, find it! You can't just create a world with no real purpose. That's not fair. There *has* to be an ending. I can't be suffering for nothing."

I'm sorry, Hope.

"You're a shit writer." Hope sat and took another swig of tequila.

The Voice didn't answer.

Drunk, disappointed, and newly aware that her world was nothing but a work of fiction, Hope fumbled with her cell phone and returned the last missed call.

CHAPTER 24

— · —

THE CALL FOR HELP

"Hope?" Mona's voice was tinged with worry. "I've been trying to reach you for weeks. You alright? How'd things go with Donna?"

"Sorry, I've been...I'm...I'm drunk. I shouldn't have called."

There were a few moments of silence before Mona responded, "It's ok, love. What's going on? Are you alone?"

"I am." Hope took another swig of tequila.

"Where are you?"

"In a storage unit. On Pine Boulevard."

"A storage unit—?"

"And guess what?" Hope sighed. "You were right about the book."

"What's the name of the storage space?"

"U-Topia Storage. Mona, I have to tell you...I'm intimidated by you."

"Hope—"

"It's true," Hope sighed. "But I'm sure you were just written that way."

"I'm coming to pick you up." Hope could hear keys jingling and a car's engine roaring to life in the background. "Give me fifteen minutes, and I'll be right there."

Hope laid back on her blanket, staring up at the metal ceiling as her vision blurred and sharpened and blurred again. Emotionally exhausted and weighed down by alcohol, Hope nodded off, drifting into the darkness of her tequila-induced slumber. She didn't hear what Mona said last. But given the level of worry in her voice, and Hope's anxiety, it was probably better that she didn't.

CHAPTER 25

— · —

CONQUER THE WORKPLACE

H ope opened her eyes and took in her surroundings as the room spun around her. She was folded into a comforter on a bed that wasn't hers and wearing silky, expensive feeling pajamas that also weren't hers. Tall floor-to-ceiling windows bathed her in a blinding, warm sunlight that stung her eyes. Abstract art hung from every wall. Her purse laid open on the nightstand next to her, with *How To Be A Better Adult* peeking out.

Hope sat up in a panic, searching for her cell phone. The day before felt like a dream. Or more like a nightmare. She hoped that it was.

It wasn't. And you're right, I'm a shit writer. The Voice sighed.

"Hey, sweetheart! Glad you finally woke up. How're you feeling?"

Hope shook away the Voice and looked up to see Mona gracefully strutting towards her, wearing a plush robe and holding a wine glass filled with water.

"My head's throbbing." Hope groaned, mortified that Mona had seen her in a drunken stupor for a second time.

"I bet." Mona laughed. She handed Hope the glass. "You're not much of a drinker."

Hope shook her head.

"You should've answered my calls." Mona sat beside Hope, laying a comforting hand on her thigh. "I was so worried."

Worried? Hope looked up at Mona, wondering what the Voice's intentions were when writing her into the plot. Was Hope simply meant to serve as a foil to Mona's perfect, graceful existence? To be taunted by her beauty and success until she somehow learned to mimic her confidence?

"Why? What makes you care so much about me?" Hope asked, hoping for more of an understanding of the plot. "I'm just a loser with no future."

"You have a future," Mona answered, "And I want to be part of it."

Hope's heart fluttered in her chest. "I-in what way?"

"In whatever way you'll allow me." Mona leaned forward and lowered her voice. "You're the only person I've met that I can't read." She pulled a lighter and a freshly rolled joint from her robe's breast pocket, then lit it as she inhaled. "Life is meaningless when you know where every step will lead you." She exhaled, blowing smoke out through her nostrils. "I've realized its uncertainty that makes life worth living. Gives people hope, gives them purpose and shit. That's why I need you. And, being beautiful helps." Mona smiled. Hope blushed.

Hope had always considered herself to be marginally attractive. Nothing to write home about, but still easy enough on the eyes to glide under the radar. She would've accepted "cute" or "adorable", but beautiful was a label she wasn't used to. She wanted to contest, to tell Mona she wasn't beautiful or mysterious and that she couldn't give her life meaning. She wanted to explain that she was nothing more than a puppet being pulled along on a string by an incompetent author. That they were fictional characters, and their lives had no inherent meaning beyond a stranger's pen and paper. Instead, she leaned in and asked, "Can I kiss you?" To which Mona replied, "I've been hoping you would."

Hope closed her eyes, pressing her lips against Mona's, tasting her marijuana-tinged breath. It was a very bold move for Hope to make, but with nothing left to lose, not her material possessions nor her sense of reality, she thought she ought to try something she hadn't before—following her heart.

Mona, smoke still billowing from the joint in her hand, tugged at the waist sash holding her robe together, letting it gracefully unfurl and fall from her shoulders. She turned and put her joint out on her bedside table while Hope's lips traveled from her face to her neck. Mona reached up and unbuttoned Hope's pajama top, sliding it off her body before drawing her closer.

As their bodies melted into one another, the two stared into each other's eyes. Mona, reveling in the unknown, and Hope, wondering if maybe every failure was worth experiencing this very moment in time.

"Were we meant to be together?" Hope asked the Voice.

I can't say it's what I intended, but it feels right, doesn't it? The Voice answered.

"I don't know. Which feels strange to say," Mona answered simultaneously, unable to hear the Voice, "But it feels right, doesn't it?"

□□□

After several hours Hope laid her head on Mona's chest as the two embraced, lying together in the folds of her comforter.

Marijuana smoke swirled in the air above them, filtering the atmosphere in a dreamy haze.

"What if I told you none of this was real? That we're just...characters in a story," Hope asked.

"Girl, you must be higher than a kite." Mona laughed.

"No, well, I don't know, maybe," Hope did feel particularly light-headed from the second-hand smoke, "but I mean it. What if this is all just...fiction?"

"Feels real to me." Mona shrugged. "Anything beyond that is none of my business."

"Hm." Mona's answer was enough to keep Hope's existential crisis at bay for the time being. Whether she was the figment of someone else's imagination or not, she existed. And life continued on, even if she wasn't always in control of how it did.

"You wanna know something?" Mona continued, "You've changed my future. Don't know how, but I can't see it anymore. Just a gaping black hole." Mona laughed, but in the way you laugh when you're relieved. "So maybe you did rub off on me."

"What was it before?" Hope asked, nervous that she'd ruined Mona's future by sharing the Voice's revelation.

Mona grimaced at the memory of her almost-inevitable future. She quickly took a draw from her joint, inhaling then blowing a cloud of smoke in Hope's direction.

"I'd like to share my past instead—if that's alright with you, love."

Hop nodded.

"A few years ago, I was right where you are. Living in a spare room with two roommates. Didn't have more than a couple hundred dollars to my name." Mona fluffed her fingers through Hope's hair. "I couldn't predict the future then."

"So how'd you climb your way out?" Hope looked up at Mona with admiration, hoping to gain any insight to apply to her own life.

"Applied for a scholarship, got a Master's in Future Studies. That's when I started noticing the patterns. I could see who was destined to make it in life and who wasn't. What kind of person was walked all over, and what kind of person commanded the room. When I saw that, I knew what I had to do." She paused as she remembered something. "After that, I watched my future change before my eyes. But I changed, too."

Mona gently stroked Hope's chin as she continued. "I started seeing people as pawns and shit. It felt so wrong. Still does. But that's how everyone plays the game. It's not right."

The infamous game. The one with rules Hope had never been privy to. If people were pawns, then Hope was stuck on the board, useless and forgotten.

"What would you rather be doing? Instead of playing the game?" Hope asked.

"I'd paint. I was an artist before all this futurist bullshit. I even had some work hung in a local gallery. But painting on canvases doesn't pay the bills."

Hope's heart sank. Just like Amber, Mona was stuck in the "adult" system, following a script that she wasn't passionate about but could follow all the same. Something Hope had failed at time and time again.

"Could I make a suggestion?" Hope called out to the Voice, hoping it was still around.

Sure, that could be helpful, the Voice answered.

"What's up?" Mona answered, unaware of the omnipresent being in Hope's head.

"Let go of the pressure of a perfect ending. Just...let the story unfold. However it's meant to."

The Voice was silent, but Hope imagined it was thinking.

"That was so poetic, love." Mona held Hope's hand in hers. "Let's plan to leave the city and start life over without all this bullshit. Create our own futures...together."

Hope recoiled from the pressure. She was fond of Mona, more so than anyone she'd ever met, but running away together wasn't quite the ending she had in mind for herself.

What is *the ending you have in mind, Hope?*

"I don't want to run away." Hope shook her head in thought. "I want to go back and balance the scales."

"You wanna move back home?" Mona asked, confused.

"No, I want to go back to W&H and put up a fight. Stand up for myself. Finally move my piece on the game board." Hope stood to retrieve her book from her bag. "And this book is going to give me the guidance I need."

Hope, trusting that the Voice would provide her with another all-knowing chapter, opened *How to Be a Better Adult.* Sure enough, what was once a blank page was now covered in printed text.

Conquer The Workplace

Have you been climbing the corporate ladder, or just hanging from its bottom rung, feet swinging over a raging sea like a child stuck on the monkey bars? I've been there. And I spent far too long hanging on that ladder, waiting for a "real" adult to come fetch me. As you can imagine, no one came.

Simply showing up to a place of employment with starched slacks and a freshly pressed button-up isn't enough to navigate through shark-infested corporate waters. Just existing will earn you another useless addition stamped onto your resume, and maybe you'll find another job just to be thrown overboard all over again.

When you're an adult, what you do becomes who you are. And why be forgettable when you can be formidable? No more clamoring to climb those rusted, uneven bars. Toughen up, buttercup. Now that you've fought Fear and found the treasure hidden beneath the Earth's surface, it's time to set sail for familiar lands, plant your flag, and conquer the workplace instead.

ACTION ITEM: *Conquer the workplace*

Conquer the Workplace. A feeling of clarity and purpose washed over Hope. She finally had a clear plan of action for her next steps. She wasn't meant to repeat the same cycle of inequity in new, uncharted lands. Nor wait as the law painfully crawled on. She was meant to play the game. To return to William Hensley & Associates and take what was rightfully hers. And, according to *How to Be a Better Adult*, all she needed was a formidable flag to plant.

Mona grabbed the book from Hope's hands and read through the chapter. "Planting a flag? You're really gonna do this?"

"Of course I am." Hope took the book back and tucked it inside her purse.

"I'm not judging you, love, I just—even if you did walk in there and give them a piece of your mind, then what? Corporate types never let up. You'd just have *another* problem on your hands. Trust me, I've seen it happen."

"Well, I've never gotten the chance to. I want to know what it feels like to command a room."

"You should really talk to Donna first. Do things the right way. That perceived power shit isn't worth it."

"I'm happy you've had this epiphany, but I personally can't afford to muse over morals or wait for the law—I have storage rent to pay."

"I can help you with that. What is it, like one hundred a month?"

"No. I *need* to do this." Hope shook her head.

A look of confusion, followed by disappointment, washed over Mona's face before she shook it away. "If this is what you need to do to be happy, go for it."

Hope looked up at Mona expectedly. "Have you seen anything in W&H's future at all? Something that might help me get a leg up?"

"You didn't hear this from me, but," Mona sighed and averted her eyes as she spoke, "there's a huge diversity issue they're trying to get ahead of. It'll be a PR nightmare for a while, but after some time, they'll just stop trying. Because no one *really* cares anyway. They'll care more about an office sex scandal that's about to come to light."

"I see." Hope thought of Alex and Monica. "Nothing about me?"

"Nothing."

"Well, at the very least, we know my mission will be inconsequential in the grand scheme of things."

"If the mission is inconsequential, why go through with it at all?"

"I've lost all there is to lose. And it started with that job. I need to go back, if not for the sake of fairness, then simply based on the principle. Every good story ends at the beginning."

"I thought this was *our* story..." Mona, slightly deflated, muttered under her breath.

Hope, oblivious to Mona's sinking mood, asked, "Could Kline Turner advise W&H about me? Maybe you could tell them it's in their best interest to concede when I arrive?"

"I can't do that, especially without seeing the outcome beforehand. I can't stand none of these folks, but I still gotta work with them come Monday morning."

"You want to embrace the unknown, don't you? Here's your chance. And if my future's truly unknown, then you'd be the only Futurist on your team with this kind of insight. It could be the leverage you'd need to move up the ranks *without* blackmailing your boss."

Mona's heart sank into her chest as Hope spoke. She recognized the kind of sleazy corporate bargaining tactic she was using on her—she'd perfected it herself over the years. But she was still so enamored with Hope and didn't want to disappoint.

"Ok, I'll see what I can do."

"Thank you," Hope kissed Mona on the forehead. "I appreciate the help, and I'll repay you, I promise."

CHAPTER 26

— · —

THE CRAFT STORE

Hope spent three dollars on a bus ride to *Bits 'N Bobs*—a crafting store that attracted both stay-at-home mothers and elderly retirees like bees to rustic-themed honey. Hope maneuvered around a gaggle of mothers in knit cardigans through an aisle of blank canvases and oil paints.

The aisle before, peppered with graying women of various heights, was dedicated to stickers and scrapbooking material. She had no feel for whether she was growing any closer to or any further away from where she needed to be. She wasn't sure what to make of any of the materials before her.

As Hope sorted through cans of paint and liquid gold, she spotted an older woman with a swirl of white hair charging through the store as if on a time-sensitive mission. Her yellow vest and walkie-talkie marked her as a craft store employee.

"Excuse me, ma'am? Where can I find wooden flagpoles?" Hope asked.

The woman glanced at Hope but continued on.

Hope followed, determined to complete her flag. "Ma'am?"

"I'm sorry, hun, but there's a little boy making a mess of the yarn aisle, and I just don't have the time." She soldiered on with Hope trailing behind her.

"I get that you're busy, and I'm sorry to interrupt, but could you please just tell me what aisle I can find flagpoles? It's for a very important project."

The older woman whipped around. "I said I don't have the time."

Remembering her goal of standing up for herself, Hope stood her ground.

"But you've just stopped. And in all this time, you could have just let me know the aisle number."

"If you think you could do a better job managing time here than me, then I suggest you put in an application, sit down for an interview, and get your own yellow vest. Until then, wait your turn to be assisted."

The white-haired woman whipped around and continued on her journey, leaving Hope to recoil from embarrassment into the nearest aisle—wall decor. The very aisle that housed the wooden flag poles. Too pleased with her find to waste another thought on the old woman's snippiness, Hope continued on to locate a tapestry.

At the end of her harrowing trek through the land of yarn and acrylic paints, thanks to the reams of coupons she'd been handed by the cashier herself, Hope only spent about forty-two dollars in total. She was beaming with pride as she tottered out of the craft store with two giant bags of supplies. And although she knew she'd been in the store for a considerable amount of time, she wasn't expecting to see a familiar brown flag billowing in the wind outside, propped up against a tiny table. Hope's heart dropped.

Within seconds she was swarmed by Troop #570.

"Miss!" Lindsey chirped. "What ya got there?"

"That's gotta be at least a-hundred dollars worth of stuff." Tasha chimed in.

"Would you like to donate today?" Sofia pushed past the two girls with her clipboard in hand.

"Donate? I *saw* you reach your goal the other day. My friend Mona gave you four-hundred dollars?"

"*That* was for our trip to Bird Lake, *now* we're raising money for upgraded uniforms." Sofia tapped on the clipboard impatiently. "We can't be seen in the same pleated skirts and boring berets as last year."

Hope's ears grew warm from the mounting pressure. "Listen, I may not have money right now," She looked down at the bags in her hands, "but I *do* have a fun arts and crafts project for you girls."

"What's the project?" Sofia asked.

"I need a battle flag. Something as pleasing to the eye as that." Hope motioned towards the brown flag next to their table. "But much more formidable. Do you know what "formidable" means?"

Sofia nodded her head.

"Excellent. Can you make it for me?"

"Depends. What do we get out of this deal?"

"I'll be using the flag to conquer my former place of employment. If all goes as planned, which I know it will, I'll fund your new uniforms." Hope was proud of her ability to both placate the young girl and outsource a bothersome task.

"Let me chat with the other girls for a sec." Sofia and the other two girls huddled together, speaking in hushed whispers, with Tasha letting out the occasional squeal.

"Ok." Sofia looked up at Hope. "We'll accept your proposition but on one condition."

"I'm all ears."

"We wanna be there when you stick the flag in the ground."

"Ah, no-can-do, this is adult business—"

"Part of our Scout Training covered hostile takeovers. Do you know what that means?"

"Of course I do." Hope hadn't the slightest clue what that meant.

"Great. So you know if you're playing dirty, you have to look the part," Sofia's eyes flicked up and down, examining Hope. "And you don't really have that vibe. No offense."

"None taken," Hope sighed.

"We want our new uniforms. You want to take over your old job. Let us come with you to make sure it happens."

"Fine. But make sure your parents are ok with this."

"They will be. You got a business card?"

"Erm, no. But I can write down my info on your clipboard-"

"What kind of adult doesn't have a business card?"

"The unemployed kind."

"Our scout leader says *every* grown-up should have at least seven streams of income."

"*Right*, of course. I'll work on that." Hope wrote out her name and phone number on Sofia's clipboard. "If you need my input for anything, you can text me here. We'll be meeting at my old job Monday morning, ok?".

"Got it!" The three scouts saluted in unison.

CHAPTER 27

— ◦ —

THE TAKEOVER

It was the crack of dawn on a Monday morning when Hope and her company of scouts arrived at William Hensley & Associates. Hope had taken the bus, and the girls were dropped off in an SUV manned by a portly woman with tousled hair and a look of worry that seemed permanently plastered on her face. As the girls excitedly slid out one-by-one in their uniforms, with red face paint smeared across their cheeks, the woman eyed the ominously glowing office building.

"You girls sure you're supposed to be here?" The woman asked Sofia.

Sofia sighed, pulling the flag out of the van's trunk. "Yes, mom. This is for our leadership badge. Remember?"

Sofia's mother looked at Hope now, who fidgeted with the watch on her wrist. "And who are you again?"

Hope opened her mouth to speak, then realized anything she said that was even close to the truth would sound insane, but she didn't have the heart to lie either. So she just replied, "I'm Hope."

"Hm."

Sofia interjected, "Moooom, I already told you she directs career day here." She lowered her voice. "You're embarrassing us."

Her mother's face softened, and she sighed. "Ok, well, I'll be back here during my lunch break. Be ready at noon sharp, ok?"

Sofia nodded her head.

"Ok, girls. Be safe and have fun!"

The two other girls stood tall and straight, responding in perfect unison as if it were a line they had practiced a million times before.

"We will, Mrs. Edozie."

Sofia's mother gave Hope one last hesitant look before slowly driving away.

Sofia handed the flag to Hope. "Ok, time to get to work."

"Time to work! Time to work!" Tasha chanted while skipping around in a circle. Her sash bobbed up and down as she hopped.

Hope took the flag and planted the wooden pole firmly into the ground. She stepped back, hands on hips, to admire the scout's handiwork. The wind whipped the black fabric to and fro, revealing a painted white skull and a pattern of bright red handprints. It was a decorative touch suggested by Sofia, who imagined it would show the higher-ups that they meant business.

Sofia stood by Hope's side, mimicking her pose. "It looks perfect. Doesn't it?"

"Well, it's the most interesting war flag I've ever seen. That's for certain" It was true. By all accounts, Hope had never seen another flag that captured the eye quite like the one that flew before her.

"The handprints are a nice touch, right?" Sofia beamed.

"They are a nice touch." Hope agreed although she thought it to be a bit too gaudy.

"So what now?" Lindsey gently tugged on Hope's sleeve. The lenses in her thick coke bottle frames glinted in the light of the building.

"Now, we wait."

□□□

Thirty-seven minutes passed before the first slew of employees arrived, their crisp slacks ironed straight to perfection and their designer shirts and blouses wrinkle-free. In their hands, they held briefcases and coat jackets. Hope held her breath as she watched the army of suits approach. She exhaled as they sluggishly walked past her, their pale, sun-starved faces emotionless and empty. She couldn't believe she'd once been part of the horde herself.

"Hello?" Tasha stamped her feet and waved her arms about in an attempt to grab the zombies' attention. No one paid her any mind.

"How strange." Lindsey crossed her arms as she watched them file into the glass building.

Eleven more minutes passed before Susan arrived, trudging up towards the door from the parking garage as if she were Atlas, with the weight of the world on her shoulders. Unlike the others who came before her, her slacks were ill-fitting, and her salt and pepper pixie cut had awkwardly grown out. As she approached, her owlish eyes took in the scene before her. The girls huddled around Hope's body.

"Well, what do we have here?" she chirped.

Hope stepped forward.

"What we have here is a hostile takeover." Hope proudly recalled the term learned from Sofia. "According to property law, this building belongs to me. So, I demand to speak to William Hensley and his board of directors."

"Or?"

"Or...we'll have to escalate the nature of our conquest from a somewhat peaceful endeavor to an uncomfortable nuisance."

"I see we've gotten a bit bold since our firing, haven't we? Do we even know what a hostile takeover is?"

"Well, erm." Hope fidgeted with her watch. In all her preparation, she had forgotten to research the term.

"Of course she does." Sofia stepped forward. "But she doesn't have any money. So this is the next best thing. Are you gonna take us to the boss man or not?"

Susan bent over to meet Sofia's stare. "And who are we?"

"You talk funny." Tasha giggled.

"We're Blossom Scouts," Sofia answered proudly. "And we're here to support Ms. Hope in her conquest. We're trained in all modes of combat. Including corporate."

"And who, may I ask, trained us?" Susan's eyes gleamed with amusement.

"Oluchi Wingrave."

Susan stood straight up and smoothed the wrinkles in her slacks with her palms. "What exactly is our relationship with Mrs. Wingrave?"

"She's our Troop Leader...and my aunt."

Hope was never hip to influential circles, so of course, she didn't know who Oluchi Wingrave was. However, she saw how the mention of her name knocked the wind out of Susan, and she watched on, intrigued.

"Oh, we're Mrs. Wingrave's niece? Of course. Let's see if Mr. Hensley has an opening in his schedule today, shall we? Follow me."

▯▯▯

In the lobby Susan pitter-pattered from here to there, pressing buttons, flipping switches, and shuffling papers until she finally took her place at her perch— the front desk. Hope and her company of scouts sat in the lobby, watching hordes of suits sidle by.

"Hey, what's the deal with your aunt?" Hope whispered.

"What?" Sofia asked.

After a year of working on the third floor of W&H, Hope had become a little too well-versed in the art of whispering.

"Sorry," she raised her voice a bit. "What's the deal with your aunt?"

"Oh, she's like super rich and important. Every time I mention her, grown-ups get weird."

"So...why doesn't *she* pay for your uniforms?"

"She would if we didn't raise enough. I just want to do something on my own for once, you know?"

Hope nodded, admiring the girl's entrepreneurial spirit.

"What's going on here?"

A tall shadow cast over Hope. She glanced up, only to see her former manager towering over her small, seated frame once again. *Chest high, chin up,* she thought. She sat up, taking note of her posture. *Remember, she's not your boss. You're here for business,* the Voice added. Hope nodded. She was thankful for the added encouragement.

"Hello, Liz."

"Her skin is so pale!" Tasha blurted out, with her finger pointed up at Liz. Lindsey rushed to muffle her mouth with her hand before she could say any more.

Liz ignored the children. "You've been terminated. You're not allowed on these premises."

Hope shrank a bit in her seat. The venom in Liz's voice was even more potent than she remembered.

"Well, I—"

Liz held up a single bony finger, silencing Hope, then turned to Susan, who nervously evaded eye contact. "Isn't it *your* job to monitor who comes and goes?"

"Yes, of course!" Susan chirped, "It's company policy to bar terminated employees from entering the building. But I believe Mr. Hensley would have a great interest in meeting with Oluchi Wingrave's niece." Susan lowered her voice to a very audible whisper. "We've been trying for ages to secure a meeting with the Wingrave's, as we know."

Liz slowly turned, finally acknowledging the Blossom Scouts. "Which of you is related to Mrs. Wingrave?"

Lindsey and Tasha pointed in unison at Sofia. Sofia clutched her sash and sat up tall, with all the confidence she could muster, as Liz slowly leaned forward, making direct eye contact with her.

"Prove it." Liz hissed. "Call her right now."

Sofia shook her head. "You wanna talk to her, you take us to Mr. Hensley."

Liz scoffed, directing her gaze back at Susan. "If you value your job, I'd suggest you call security and have these pests escorted off the property".

Susan, taken aback, pursed her lips in a manner that could only be read as highly offended. But before she could respond, the phone on her desk began to ring. She answered, leaving the girls and Liz frozen in uncomfortable silence. Liz, wrought with impatience, crossed her arms and tapped her pointed shoes on the marble floor. Hope looked down, pulling at a loose thread in her slacks.

"Uh-huh, yeah, uh huh. Yes, it is." Susan twirled the phone cord as she spoke to whoever was on the other line. "Yes, ok. I see. And did they mention anything about Oluchi Wingrave, by chance? Ah ok. Yes, her niece is here in the lobby." There was a long pause before she followed up with, "Sure, I'll let everyone know." She hung up, her eyes full of secrets that everyone in the room knew she couldn't keep.

"That was Legal on the ninth floor. They've received word about our little predicament here from Kline Turner Solutions."

A smile spread across Hope's face. Mona must have done her part.

"And? They want them removed, correct? " Liz checked her beeping smartwatch. "Can we end this nuisance now? I need to check on my employees."

"Well, that can certainly be done without us, can't it?" Susan flashed a satisfied smile, "Because Mr. Hensley would like to meet with our guests. Alone."

A flush of color came to Liz's grey skin. She cleared her throat to hide her embarrassment.

"Well, I anticipate hearing all about this waste of time during our next all-floor management meeting." Liz shot daggers at Hope with her eyes before stepping into the open elevator, "And continually breaking company policy is a surefire way to ruin your reputation in this industry. I'll make sure of that." The elevator doors slid closed, consuming Liz and all her poison.

□□□

"She's such a witch, that one." Susan shook her head and stood to her feet, motioning for the girls to follow her. "I've heard she's in the middle of a nasty divorce. Her poor husband was miserable. He's taking everything, even the kids. But she deserves it."

Hope couldn't imagine a woman like Liz having children. But with her cold demeanor and micro-managing tendencies, it was easy to imagine her husband shouting, "I can't take it anymore!" while throwing his belongings into a U-haul. And even still, Hope felt sorry for the woman. Maybe she threw herself into her work to escape her lonely reality at home. Maybe her only source of control in life came from the third floor reaching their acquisition and retention quota every month. *Or maybe it doesn't matter, because going through something gives you no right to toss your misery onto everyone else,* the Voice added.

"Hm, you're absolutely right," Hope responded.

"Happy you agree," Susan answered, not realizing Hope was speaking to no one.

Susan veered right and led the group behind a pair of double doors, down a dimly lit corridor that seemed to jump back in time with each step. The marble floor became worn hardwood, with wooden molding on the walls to match. With one turn, the bright white walls yellowed, chipped, and peeled.

"Scary," Tasha whimpered while clinging to Lindsey's arm. Sofia put on a brave face, but Hope noticed her eyes darting about, taking in every crevice, every shadow, and chasing after every sound.

After some time, they arrived at a vintage-looking elevator lift. The kind guarded by iron fencing. One that would need to be operated by hand.

"This is the only way up to the tenth floor," Susan explained. "Mr. Hensley enjoys his privacy."

Hope eyed the copper crank, then looked back at Susan's short, feeble-looking arms.

"You'll be operating this thing?"

"Yes, and go on, quickly. So I can return to my desk."

Hope, Sofia, Lindsey, and Tasha reluctantly entered the elevator car. Susan slid the iron fence shut behind them.

"Please keep our hands and feet to ourselves. We wouldn't want anyone else losing a finger," Susan warned.

"Anyone...*else*?" Hope nervously asked.

"Up we go!" Susan threw the weight of her body into the crank, pushing it forward, over, and under until the car slowly groaned upward.

The Blossom Scouts gathered around Hope, holding on to her for dear life, Sofia included. Hope held the girls tight, willing Susan's strength to persevere through all nine floors. The elevator slid up past floors three, four, and five, lighting up each corresponding number on the inner panel. Hope held her breath as they passed eight and nine and finally ended on ten. The car stopped moving.

"Alright! Looks like you've made it!" Susan's shrill voice echoed up through the shaft. "Go down the hall, then take a left, then a right! He'll be waiting for you!"

CHAPTER 28

— • —

THE LIFE OF WILLIAM HENSLEY

William "Willy" Hensley was born to a single mother in a small city in the Northeast. He was the first of nine children, each with a different absentee father whose surnames they took on as their own.

With his small frame, quiet presence, and less-than-humble beginnings, Willie was taunted by his schoolmates, who'd call out "Little Willy" and "Whispering Will" when he'd shuffle by. After bursting into tears because he just couldn't take it, they modified their taunts, and poor Willy Hensley became "Wah-Wah Willie" for the rest of his time in school.

After graduating high school, Willy's mother couldn't afford to put him through University. So, Willy went to work. He sauntered from door to door, asking each business to please hire him. He'd tell them he was an honest man, looking for honest work. Each and every business slammed their doors in Willy's face.

When he was nineteen, his mother fell ill and died, leaving his eight younger siblings in his care. Willy was devastated by his mother's passing, but a small part of him was relieved. His mother was free, and her life insurance would be very useful. Willy sat across from the insurance agent, laying a hand on his knee to stop his leg from shaking. For weeks he'd anticipated the amount, and daydreamed about all the ways he'd spend each dollar. But he was horrified to hear the truth.

"Well, son, looks like you're not entitled to any of your old lady's money."

"What? No. Look, I brought all the documents—" Willy pulled a crumpled death certificate from his pocket and dug for his own birth certificate.

The agent held up his hand to spare him any further embarrassment. "I'm sorry, but there's a will. And the beneficiary on this account is Barron Hensley."

Willy's jaw dropped. Barron was the father he had never met. The father who ran off to continue "making a name for himself". The father who missed every single one of his nineteen birthdays. He missed so much that Willy assumed he was dead.

"Why, why would she do that?" Willy asked, desperate to make sense of his mother's choices.

"Listen, I don't know your mother. But seems like she didn't have her stuff in order. Sorry kid."

Willy stuffed his mother's death certificate back into his pocket and left the insurance agency. He ambled down the street and ambled into a bar and spent his last buying a copious amount of booze. As he grew more intoxicated, his quiet voice grew louder. Soon he was spinning tall tales to the patrons of the bar, who watched and listened in awe with eyes glazed over by the effects of alcohol.

One of these patrons was a hefty man in a pinstripe suit with a lit cigar hanging from his mouth. The man was Charles Day, the city's most successful business owner...and its most ruthless criminal. Charles approached Willy when the crowd began to disperse and asked about his claim that he tripled the sales of a foreign business owner's perfumery.

Willy, still drunk, recounted the whole story. It wasn't a true story by any means, but the truth doesn't matter when people believe hard enough. And Charles believed. Willy was hired on the spot as Charles' advisor. Even in his drunken stupor, Willy knew it was an offer he couldn't refuse. Not that he would anyway—he needed the money. He shook Charles' blood-soaked hand and became his right-hand man and confidant.

Willy soon learned that honest work led to nothing but struggles and dream-chasing. It was only through deception that he saw a change in his life. With each lie he told, his pockets grew larger, and soon he was swimming in dough.

Charles eventually died at the hands of a rival gangster, but not before handing Willy a hefty stack of cash.

"You're great at what you do, Willy. You've done me and my businesses good. Take this, and start your own business."

With Charles' blessing and his large investment, Willy acquired a towering ten-floor building in the South. He wanted to start fresh in a new city where there were no traces of "Wah-Wah Willy" left. William Hensley and Associates is what he called his endeavor. There were no associates, only William and his dozens of employees, but he thought the name sounded particularly professional.

For many years the company published a newspaper recalling all the city's happenings—the Daily Day. Writers would be encouraged to spin tales and jumpstart rumors in order to increase their readership. It worked, but after being hit with several defamation lawsuits, the firm pivoted to marketing and sales. While media can be fickle, every business needs help amplifying its messaging to the world. And William Hensley knew selling tales was his expertise.

As he grew more absentminded with deep wrinkles drawn into his face, William knew he needed an heir to take on his dynasty of lies and deceit. He met a lovely young woman named Tara while she served him drinks at a gentleman's bar and paid her to spend the night with him. She fell pregnant and gave birth to his son William Hensley II.

Willy was overjoyed to have a son and vowed to be a better father than his deadbeat dad. He instilled the idea of lying your way to the top into his tiny son, or, he tried to. Will Jr. was a rebellious teen with a troubling honesty streak. Willy did everything he could to turn him to a life of deception, but nothing he did or said could convince him. And one day, while crafting an email, lying to his employees about their bonuses, he died.

Will Jr. was lying on a beach in Bora Bora when he received the call. He scrunched up his face and sighed. "Aw, man. You mean I gotta be a CEO now?"

Chapter 29

The CEO

Will Jr's office still held remnants of his father. The dark wooden paneling on the exceptionally high walls. The thick velvet drapes that lined the windows. The towering desk, meant to intimidate all who stepped foot into the owner's chamber. And his literal remains, contained in a ceramic urn, that he requested be kept in a glass case so he may remain ever-present in all business dealings. But as the years wore on and Will Jr. settled into his forced role as CEO, he added a few of his own touches.

Right in front of his desk sat a space-themed foosball table, where little metal men played futuristic soccer. Against the back wall was a row of brightly lit arcade games. And there was a snack-filled vending machine that didn't actually take money but was re-stocked daily, so Will Jr. could have a taste of what he considered to be an average life.

"Would you girls like some snacks?" he asked.

When the girls entered the office Will Jr. was perched on his foosball table, holding a stapled document and wearing a relaxed dress shirt tucked into jeans—not slacks. His face was innocent and kind, with deep smile lines and gleaming brown eyes that were rimmed with sleep. Even so, he didn't look a day over thirty-five.

He was far from the aging, bearded overlord that Hope had imagined. But having been deceived by a friendly face in the past, she remained vigilant.

"Snacks!" Tasha squealed. She took a step forward to accept Will's proposition but was stopped by Lindsey, who grabbed the back of her sash, keeping her anchored in place.

"In our Blossom Scout's handbook, it states that as exceptional young women existing in a not-so-kind world, it's in our best interest to not accept snacks of any kind from strangers." Lindsay recited as Sofia looked on proudly.

Will Jr. laughed. "No problem at all. I get it. You're here for serious business, after all." He hopped off the foosball table. "So, I've been informed that it's in *my* best interest to hear what you have to say. It's Hope, right?" He extended a hand to Hope, which she firmly shook.

"That's correct. Pleasure to meet you, Mr. Hensley."

"Call me Will. Mr. Hensley was my father." He motioned towards the urn before laughing to himself. "Terrible guy, honestly."

"I'm sorry."

"So am I. Anyway, I've been given an Order of Business from the Board." He held up the document in his hands. "Order of Business" was printed on the cover page in large, bold letters. "I'm sure they're having a great time watching this meeting." He motioned towards a tiny camera affixed to the wall, pointing down at the group.

"Apparently, they don't trust me with serious matters such as..." he flipped through the document, "ah such as *this*. So before we discuss Mrs. Wingrave, Hope, I've been informed by our lawyers that you've found a contract, stating that you allegedly own our property?"

"Yes, that's correct. I found it in my backyard."

"In your *backyard*? Like some sort of time capsule?" Will laughed. "I'm sure my father's powdery remains are rolling in his urn right now," His cell phone vibrated. He answered, wiping the grin from his face. "Hello? Ah, ok, right. Sorry, won't happen again." Will glanced up at the cameras before continuing. "We're contesting the validity of the document, and this feeble attempt at a corporate takeover will be noted and used in support of our case."

"Actually," Sofia stepped forward before Hope could answer, "It states in your own company handbook that challenging upper management is both celebrated *and* invited. So using this clear exercise of that right to challenge you as a negative stain on Hope's character would be misaligned with your company's values."

Hope was impressed. Sofia had done her homework.

"Hm, that is in the handbook, isn't it?" Will thought for a moment. "Well, fair is fair—" Will's cell phone vibrated again, which he answered. "Yes, uh huh. Well, actually, I feel it makes sense. Ok, sure, but who's the CEO, me or you? Sure, alright." Will shook his head. "The Board says we do not have to operate within the bounds of our company handbook. The lawyers say it will never hold up in court."

"Listen," Hope—frustrated, exhausted, and sick of the back and forth—spoke up, "in the year I worked here, I gained no transferable skills, was paid below a living wage, and was overlooked and bullied by HR and management. Even if you don't think this takeover is serious, the lawsuit I'll be raising will be."

Hope was bluffing, of course, but as she flipped through the files tucked away in her mind, she recalled bits of leverageable information.

"As you know," she continued, "my lawyer's Donna Choi, and as you've seen...I know how to make headlines. When the curtain gets pulled back on your diversity issue, unfair practices, and unlawful terminations, it'll be a PR hailstorm for you all."

"That sounds horrible," Will Jr. leaned on his foosball table, deep in thought, ignoring the increasingly aggressive vibration of his cell phone. "I'm sorry you had to deal with that here."

"*Sounds* horrible? It's your company. You know it's horrible."

Will shook his head. "When they're not locking me in this office, they're touting me around as the face that gets the blame when things go south. I don't know what's going on beyond what they," he pointed at the camera, "tell me."

"Well, have they told you that Liz Morton makes third-floor employees work in the dark?"

"Oh, that? Yeah, of course. She's just sensible. Saves us a ton of money on our light bill."

Hope shook her head in confusion. "You don't think there's a problem with employees squinting in the dark for nine hours a day?"

Will shrugged. "If you're here to work, and it helps with productivity, then no I really don't see a problem with it."

"What about the fact that Monica Minsky brings personal issues to work and wrongfully terminated me?"

"From what I have heard, you broke the terms of your employment by taking an extended lunch and sharing confidential files. And according to the company handbook, those *are* fireable offenses. Fair is fair."

"But I was given the work of *five* people."

"Obviously someone thought you were a talented employee and equipped for the job. I'm genuinely failing to see what the issue is."

Hope stood with her mouth agape in disbelief. She had nothing more to say. Just as she was about to give up, she felt a tiny tug on her sleeve. She turned to see Tasha, motioning for her to join the huddled Blossom Scouts behind her. Hope lifted her finger, signaling for Will Jr. to hold on for a moment, then lowered herself to the girls' level.

Sofia whispered, "You're drowning out there, Hope. We need a different approach."

"What were you thinking?" Hope softly whispered.

"What?"

"Sorry," Hope whispered a bit louder. "What were you thinking?"

"We have two options. Tasha can distract him while we attack from behind."

"I brought rope!" Tasha whispered, patting her satchel.

"Rope?"

"To hold him hostage," explained Lindsey.

"What's the other option?"

"I can call my aunt. She can be really intimidating," Sofia explained.

"How about we try that one first?"

"Ok, I'll video call her!"

"Aw, man." Tasha's head hung from disappointment.

The girls turned around, with Sofia leading the charge.

"Mr. Hensley. We're not too fond of how you're speaking to our friend Hope. She's been treated badly, and she's gone through every avenue she can to rectify the situation. As such, I'll be calling my aunt Oluchi to speak to you on her behalf."

"You're calling Oluchi Wingrave?"

Sofia nodded her head.

Will Jr. nervously loosened his collar and looked up into the camera.

"She's calling Oluchi Wingrave. I really think this is something for the lawyers to handle?" His cell phone vibrated, and he answered. "Yes, yes. Ok, absolutely." Will hung up the phone and slid it into his pocket. "Before you call anyone, let's take a field trip to Legal on the ninth floor, shall we?"

CHAPTER 30

— ◆ —

THE NINTH FLOOR

I f Will Hensley's office was wedged in the past, the ninth floor was thrust far into the future. There were no cubicles, no bean bag chairs, or private offices. Instead, the glass doors slid open, revealing a sterile white, brightly lit floor with a large glass table in the center of the space.

Around that table were ten plush rolling chairs, and on each chair sat a black-clad lawyer with a serious expression pasted on their face. They tapped away in almost unison on their keyboards. And when one turned their head, they all followed.

The lawyers spoke as one, "Mr. Hensley. Always a pleasure." They looked over at Hope, together. "So this is Ms. Obiako? The former employee who found the invalid contract?"

"Excuse me, the contract is very valid," Hope scoffed.

"We dispute that claim." The lawyers remained expressionless.

Will Jr. stepped in. "Yes, this is Hope, and this," he slid behind Sofia and softly grabbed her shoulders, "is Oluchi Wingrave's niece. She would like for you to speak with her."

"Please, call her. We'd love to be connected," the lawyers answered.

"Now, before I call her. I want you to know, I'll be informing her of what you've done to Hope. And she won't like it."

"Wait, don't call her."

"I'm definitely calling her."

"No," the lawyers looked at each other as if speaking through brain waves before one spoke on his own. "I'm sure we can reach some sort of equitable solution if you'd like to call your lawyer, Hope."

Chapter 31

— • —

Long Drawn-Out Meeting

LONG DRAWN-OUT PRIVATE CLOSED-DOOR MEETING.

CHAPTER 32

— · —

THE PAYBACK

After a long, drawn-out, closed-door meeting, Hope and the Blossom Scouts were escorted through the lobby by one of the Ninth Floor lawyers. He had introduced himself as "Adam" but didn't sound entirely sure of his own name. The moment he was separated from the others, Adam sort of hunched within himself, clearing the nervousness from his throat every few minutes. Hope observed him curiously, wondering how someone so meek could have climbed the ranks at a place like W&H.

The Scouts led the way, gleefully skipping in front of Adam and Hope. Tasha and Lindsey with snacks in hand, and Sofia counting a stack of cash from selling two years' worth of Blossom Scout cookies as part of their deal.

"Thank you for escorting us." Hope smiled to diffuse the awkwardness.

Adam's eyes nervously darted away.

"I've been advised not to exchange pleasantries at the risk of disclosing anything that may affect the outcome of the meeting today."

"Right. Ok then."

As the group approached Susan's perch, Hope noticed a familiar silhouette, draped in a tacky burgundy suit, leaning against the front desk, chittering with Susan. It was Monica. As she turned and caught sight of Hope, her face twisted into a look of disgust.

"Hope?" Monica's voice was as shrill as Hope remembered. "What are you doing here?" Monica's eyes shot up to Adam, then down to the smiling Scouts.

"Just been called in as a witness. Apparently, there's been a few scandals involving HR co-mingling with third-floor Account Managers in more ways than one," Hope lied. She watched with satisfaction as Monica's face slowly dropped with the weight of the realization.

"Oh?" Susan leaned over her perch, "Now, what's this about?"

Monica ignored Susan's inquiry, instead looking to Adam for answers.

"What's going on?" Her voice dropped, "Is there an investigation?"

"I cannot disclose what's been discussed."

Monica huffed and shot Hope a fiery glare before straightening her suit jacket in a poor attempt to regain her composure. "I'm sure we'll be hearing about it at the next all-floor management meeting?"

Adam cleared his throat, "Absolutely not."

Monica, visibly shaken, slithered towards the elevator. "Well, I suppose I should get going. I have work to do, seeing as I'm actually employed here."

A smile spread across Hope's face before she replied, "Not for long."

The color left Monica's face as the elevator doors closed in front of her.

□□□

"How was career day?" Sofia's mom called out to the Blossom Scouts from her SUV's window, watching as they slid their battle flag back into the car's trunk.

"It was so much fun!" Tasha jumped up and down, her little beaded braids clattering with excitement. "We sold all our cookies!"

The woman looked at Hope as Tasha and Lindsey slid into the backseat of the van.

"They can be a handful, I hope they didn't get into too much trouble."

"They were no trouble at all." Hope warmly smiled.

While the girls didn't technically cause any trouble, they *were* cunning, deceitful, and surprisingly persuasive.

"Will your aunt really work with them? They're kind of horrible." Hope had whispered to Sofia while on one of their many bathroom breaks during the long drawn-out meeting. Minutes before, Sofia had marched in front of the lawyers, screaming about them never living the day down if they didn't reach a resolution.

Sofia shrugged. "She probably won't. One thing I learned from my Auntie Oluchi is to let people believe what they want for as long as they want to get what *you* want."

Hope was alarmed and slightly disturbed but had to give credit where credit was due.

She shook Sofia's mom's hand and said, "They have a bright future ahead of them in Corporate America."

CHAPTER 33

— · —

HER TINY WORLD

Hope sat at the bus stop reflecting on how a single five-minute phone call with a "powerful" person led to more forward movement than any effort she could have ever made on her own. She really was just a player in an unfair game. And she had finally won, *really* won, but it still felt strange.

Isn't this the ending you wanted? The Voice asked.

"I'm not sure."

Hope's phone rang. It was Donna Choi.

"It's Donna. Why didn't you inform me of your relationship with Oluchi Wingrave? That's crucial information."

Hope wanted to say she had no relationship with Oluchi Wingrave, that her only connection with her was one of the children she bribed, but she didn't think it would be wise to share.

"Sorry, didn't know it was relevant."

"And you didn't call me before storming the building. They were already painting you as a disgruntled former employee. Do you know how wrong that could have gone? Next time, seek the advice of your counsel."

"Next time?"

"You've just obtained a considerable amount of money. Once people catch wind of this, there *will* be lawsuits heading your way...and I'm on retainer for the next twelve months. Don't worry, you've already paid me."

Donna continued on about Hope's increased net worth and other legal jargon that Hope didn't quite understand. As the conversation wore on, she peppered in the occasional "ah" and "I see" so Donna would think she was digesting the information. In reality, she was so mentally drained she struggled to follow along.

Hope saw her bus approaching in the distance. "Oh, Donna, we'll have to connect later, my ride's arrived, and I don't want to discuss sensitive information around the driver."

"Smart. I'll have my assistant reach out to schedule another call."

The bus rolled to a stop in front of Hope. As she stood, cell phone in hand, the doors slid open, revealing Darius sitting in the driver's seat. He looked down at Hope with a blank expression.

"Darius..."

"Good evening, ma'am."

Hope stepped on the bus, keeping her eyes on Darius. He didn't look at her but swung the doors shut as soon as she was seated. She glanced up at him through the rearview mirror, knowing he wouldn't return her friendly gaze.

"I know I messed up," Hope whimpered.

A few minutes of silence passed before Darius spoke, keeping his eyes on the road.

"I see you're back at that company. Glad things are working out for you."

Hope finally broke her gaze and looked out the window. "Are you still fighting?"

"Nope. Called it quits after I took that beating."

Hope looked back up at Darius' reflection. "No, you can't give up. You're the one who inspired me to keep trying."

"Yeah? And what happened after that?"

Hope hung her head.

Darius continued, "Some people are primed to live happy lives, knowing what they wanna be and where they wanna go, and life unfolds for them in that way. Others are doomed to a life of hardship. I was luckily destined to be average. Right in the middle. I had my glory days, and life moves on. Nothing wrong with that."

"You're not average. You're far from it."

Darius looked up to meet Hope's eyes in the rearview mirror.

"I may *look* like I have it together right now, but I'm lonelier than ever." Hope fidgeted with her wristwatch. "I can't make sense of anything on my own."

"Listen," Darius' face softened into a look of sympathy, "I know why you jumped into that ring. Same reason I did. To feel important. Like your life actually matters on the big huge rock we call a planet. But you know what I realized?"

"What?"

"All that time I spent training for that fight, trying to make my cousin's sacrifice worth it? I could've been spending that time with my mom before she passed." Darius' voice broke a little. "She died, right after that fight. And there I was chasing glory and trying to prove something instead of tending to my people and making those moments count."

"Darius, I'm so sorry." Hope's heart sank deep into her chest.

"There aren't enough sorries, not enough prayers and thoughts in the world that'll make the hurt go away." Darius shook his head as he turned the wheel. "Life is long. And random. And before you know it, you're in a place you never thought you'd be at. I'm not living in the past anymore. And I'm not getting lost in some future that doesn't exist to me yet. Simple as that. I'm staying present, and if you wanna be less lonely, I'd suggest you do the same."

Hope watched as Darius rolled to another stop, swinging open the doors to let in passengers. He greeted them one by one.

"Hey there, name's Darius. Pleasure to be driving you today." When he saw a young child hop on the bus, he added, "Hold on tight this bus is prone to taking off like a rocket ship!"

The little girl laughed, and her tired-looking mother flashed Darius a grateful smile before taking her seat.

Hope recalled Bartholemew Livingston's contract. How in his tiny world, he was displeasurable and greedy. In Darius' tiny world, he was warm and comforting. Even when he didn't need to be. Even when he had every reason to give Hope the cold shoulder. She thought of Amber, who dropped everything to see her simply because she felt moved to. Who noticed every shift and change in her mood. Who made it her mission to fill in her gaps. Hope thought of her mother, Tochi. Always opening the door for Hope to ask for help, although Hope never dared step through for fear her father would be on the other side wagging his finger in disapproval. And Mona, who allowed her the space to unzip her corporate constraints from the moment they met.

These were the people in Hope's tiny world. They poured into her simply because she existed. No negotiating necessary. No closed-door meetings. No networking. And yet, these are the people she had been neglecting.

"Ms. Hope, I believe this is your stop."

Hope looked up to see Darius and the other passengers watching her impatiently. She shook her head. "I don't live here anymore."

Darius raised his eyebrows inquisitively but didn't ask any questions. He kept on with the route. One by one, each passenger exited the bus until the only two left were Hope and Darius.

When the bus reached her stop, right in front of the rows of brown blocky buildings that made up U-Topia Storage, Darius watched as Hope stood to exit.

"You sure this is where you're supposed to get off?" he asked, his voice laced with concern.

"Yeah, just checking on my belongings. I'm moving soon." Hope cleared her throat. "I know you aren't fond of me right now. And maybe you never will, but you were my first friend in the city. I'm sorry I was so blinded by my own misery that I added to yours."

Darius turned again to look at Hope.

"It's alright." Even when grieving, the friendliness never left his eyes.

"I want to give you something—if you'll accept," Hope whispered now, pulling a folded check from her pocket and handing it to Darius. "It's addressed to me, but once I deposit it, I'd like to send you half."

Darius' eyes widened in disbelief as he unfolded the check and read the amount.

"Hope, where'd you get this from? I can't take all this."

"You deserve it. I'll wire it to you as soon as I can." Hope's voice cracked as she spoke.

"Hope—"

"Please. Please, accept it. Use it to chase another dream."

Darius examined Hope's sullen face for a few moments before speaking.

"I'd like to give you a hug if that's alright with you."

Hope nodded, unable to speak lest the tears behind her lids escaped. Darius stood to his feet, his tall body towering over Hope's. He wrapped his arms around her and held her tight.

Hope felt a warm, wet droplet hit her forehead. She looked up to see tears streaming down Darius' face. He wiped them away with the back of his hand.

CHAPTER 34

— · —

THE GOODBYE

The next morning, Hope sat on the floor of her storage unit, taking in its metal walls and concrete floors for what would be the last time. No more city living. Hope was ready to move back to her tiny hometown.

She had more than enough money to buy a house of her own, but thought it'd be more sensible to rent an apartment until she was ready for the burden of home ownership. She'd already called Amber to inform her of her impending arrival.

"Girl, are you serious? You're really moving back home?" Amber squealed. "I'll have my best friend back! You can help me with wedding planning."

I could pay for the whole thing, Hope thought. But she'd been advised by Donna Choi to keep the true nature of her elevated tax bracket a secret from those around her, lest they be targeted for lawsuits too. So instead, she said, "Of course, I'll help. Whatever you need."

"I've gotta tell Jimoh. He's gonna be so excited." Amber's voice dropped to a more serious tone. "Thanks for not giving up, Hope."

□□□

Later, Hope stared up at her bookshelf, reminiscing over each precious title she'd read over the years. She slid *How to Be a Better Adult* next to her faded orange book.

"I think I'll be leaving these books behind."

Leaving them behind? But, you love your books. The Voice sounded a bit panicked.

"I've read more self-help books than I'd like to admit—"

I know how many you've read, Hope. I created you.

"Ah, right. Well, I think I'm done being guided by books, if that's alright with you. I want to write a story of my own."

Understandable.

"I know you must think you're a lousy adult out there, especially if you created me the way you did. You really shouldn't be so hard on yourself. Ease up on the self-loathing."

I'll consider that. The Voice seemed to be fading with each word.

"And I'm sorry I called you a shit writer," Hope called out before the Voice completely disappeared.

Thunk, thunk, thunk.

There was a hollow knocking on the storage space door. Hope checked her watch. The movers were considerably early, not that it mattered. She stood to her feet, then bent down to slowly pull up the metal door.

"Mona?"

Mona stood in the door frame, dressed in a sleek, tailored suit with expensive-looking accessories. Her braids were pulled into a low ponytail and in her hand was a briefcase. Her eyes were tinted red like she'd been crying.

"Shouldn't you be at work?" Hope asked.

"I couldn't let you leave without properly saying goodbye." Mona looked down at the concrete floor. "And without telling you how I feel. Mind if I sit?" She motioned towards Hope's pile of blankets.

"Absolutely, please do."

Mona sat, and Hope plopped down next to her.

"I'm glad the conquering was a success, by the way. And thanks for the wire. You didn't have to pay me."

"Thank you for your help." Hope averted her eyes. "I—I shouldn't have used you like that. It was selfish of me to ask for so much."

"It's ok. It was presumptuous of me to try and tell you what to do. You were right. You should be able to make choices for yourself. And looks like you chose correctly." Mona hung her head in thought, or possibly sorrow.

"What are you thinking?" Hope struggled to read Mona's tone and thought it better to ask than to assume.

"I'm thinking I have feelings for you that aren't returned. At least not in the same way."

Hope remained silent. She couldn't contest, as she knew it was true. She could feel Mona's affection for her growing from a flickering flame to a raging wildfire. And while she was fond of Mona, more than anyone she'd ever met, she didn't feel the same fiery passion. At least not yet.

Mona continued, "I know what my future looks like without you. And I—if being with you can change it, it must mean something. It must mean we're meant to be together. But it's your choice."

Hope thought for a moment. She imagined what life could be with Mona in it. Waking to her warm laugh, lovingly braiding her hair, helping her break her almost alarming weed habit. With Mona, she wouldn't be alone anymore. It was a lovely future, but one that Hope wasn't ready for yet. What she needed most was the space to discover herself without the anxiety. Without the pressure to succeed. She wanted to muse and write and experience life with her newfound freedom.

"I'm sorry. I'm not ready for that kind of commitment. Not yet. But I do still want you in my life." Hope held Mona's hand. "Let's visit each other as often as we can."

Mona inhaled deeply, trying her best to maintain her composure. She cleared her throat and willed a smile to her face. "We'll definitely keep in touch, love."

Hope leaned over and kissed Mona on the cheek. Mona turned and kissed Hope on the lips. Her hand traveled down Hope's back, pulling her in closer. Hope stroked Mona's face, wiping away her tears with her thumb.

What she didn't know was Mona's future had returned, slowly materializing from a gaping black hole back to what seemed to be her inescapable fate—a warm, bright, and *absolute* ending. Mona quietly cried to herself, regretting the choices she'd made in life.

CHAPTER 35

— ⁘ —

THE END

"I'm coming home." Hope spoke to her mother on the phone as she rode the bus to the airport. She could've called for a car, of course, but she was a creature of habit and found the bus ride to be more peaceful. "I found an apartment near the house."

"Oh, that's wonderful, *ada*. We've missed you."

Hope smiled to herself. She could hear the love in her mother's voice radiating through the phone waves.

"I've missed you too."

"Peter! Your daughter's moving back home." Tochi's voice muffled as she called for Hope's father. "Yes, she's on the phone now." There were a few moments of rustling before Peter's harsh voice cut into the line.

"So you've failed," Peter scoffed. "Didn't I tell you not to move in the first place? Now you've wasted time and money."

"Peter!" Tochi snapped in the background.

"You're right. I failed to live up to your standard of what a perfect adult should be. And I failed myself by even trying to."

Peter sucked his teeth.

"I'm buying mommy a house in Nigeria," Hope continued. "You can live there too, I guess, if she lets you."

"Buying a house? With what money? Listen to me, you need to go back to school and face your books—"

Hope hung up the phone and pulled her *Journal For Hope* from her bag. She turned to the first page, clicked her pen, and began to write.

ACKNOWLEDGMENTS

Thank you to everyone in my tiny world who inspired the characters in this book. I may not have an Adult Handbook, but I feel loved by all of you.

To listen to a playlist inspired by the book, search "How To Be A Better Adult" on Spotify. To buy a manual for yourself, check out jacqueaye.com. To see Mona's future, look out for what's next.

-Jacque Aye